MITTY WALTERS
BREAKING
GRAVITY

~ MoBetter Productions Inc ~

Breaking Gravity
Published by MoBetter Productions Inc
Copyright 2014 Mitty Walters

Edited by: David Gatewood

ISBN-10: 0-692-23971-5
ISBN-13: 978-0-692-23971-1

SPECIAL THANKS TO:

Suz, my muse! Thank you for all the encouragement and for
shepherding this lost soul. I would never have finished, were it
not for you.

Uncle Charlie, the mad scientist. Thank you for tolerating me and
for not strangling me as I barraged you with emails about physics.

My pal Al, the *new* Hardest Working Man in Show Business.
Almost as funky as the OG. Thank you for inspiring me. You are
my real-life hero.

And my buddy Matt. Thank you for your words of encouragement,
and for all the deep, insightful commentary and counsel.

For my beautiful, sweet, long-suffering wife and for the three coolest little dudes on the planet.

FOREWORD
by Al Letson

For most of my adult life, I've lived partly in the world of suburban America, and partly out of a suitcase. Somehow I've managed to make a living out of what I love best: being on the road. But I'm not a fancy-hotel type traveler. Well, okay... maybe as I've gotten older, I appreciate a decent hotel. But in my youth, I spent plenty of time sleeping on friends' couches, on subway cars, and a few times on someone's doorstep (don't ask). Traveling like that, close to the ground, you meet people in a completely different way than you do if you're only interacting with the concierge or taxi driver. Living like that, I found that I'd stumbled into a uniquely American experience, and I loved it. Not just the adventure of the road, but the people: the everyday, ordinary Americans. The folks who make this country run, who get up and go to work, take care of their families, and connect with their communities. People just like you.

So what the hell does that philosophizing about ordinary people have to do with this book? Everything. *Breaking Gravity* is a lot of things—first and foremost, it's a fun adventure that grabs you by the throat early on and doesn't let go. But underneath—the bones upon which the flesh resides—it's a story about an everyday person, someone a lot like me and you, who creates something extraordinary; and *that* is a true American story. Invention! Dreams manifest! The future! When we look at the devices we use today, the creators have become these mythic figures: Steve Jobs, Henry Ford, Stan Lee (hey, I'm a comic book nerd, I had to get in one reference). Their contributions to society have shaped the way we live and the way we think, and so of course it's natural that we elevate them to icon status. But before they became icons, they, too, were everyday people. People like you, people like me. What set them apart was their ability to dream big—and actually do something about it.

In reading *Breaking Gravity*, I couldn't help but think about these issues. Have we lost our ability to dream? Have we farmed the idea of innovation to our sacred places of learning: ivory towers that only the elite can enter? Have we forgotten that at the core of every great invention is an everyday person who wasn't an icon when he started? More likely, he or she had seen more failure than success when at last one crazy idea actually worked, shifting the trajectory of their lives.

The lead character in *Breaking Gravity*, Dale Adams, comes from the same mold as all those great thinkers—*before* we thought of them as great thinkers. A kid from a rough-and-tumble background, with a curious itch that leads him to the discovery of a lifetime. I'll be honest with you: I love science, but it takes me a bit to grasp it at times, and many of the concepts in this book made me stop and rethink some of the basic truths. What is gravity? How does it work? How is it communicated? Does gravity have an opposite, and if so, how do we harness it? These are questions that push Dale and drive the narrative.

What Mitty has tapped into with this book is a deep longing that is born in the soul of us all—a desire to see what's beyond. Maybe life tramples it down, or maybe we just don't nurture it, and it goes away. But for some of us, that call stretches across obstacles, forces us to do something. I know, I know, heavy stuff to lay on a fun book filled with a lot of action, government bad guys, and conspiracies; and yet, it's there, just under the surface.

Don't worry: if you're just looking for a fun read you're in the right place. But, like the characters in this book, you might find that sometimes inspiration can come from the most unlikely sources.

+++

Al Letson is a celebrated poet, an acclaimed p. right, and the former host of *State of the Re:Union*, a nationally syndicated radio program on NPR. Currently Letson is the host of *Reveal*, a *Peabody Award* winning investigative news program on NPR.

SOUNDTRACK

For those who enjoy listening to music while they read, below is a **Suggested Playlist** for *Breaking Gravity*. No endorsements are express or implied.

For your convenience, a YouTube playlist containing the entire playlist can be found here:

www.tinyurl.com/DIYgravity

Chap 1 - Crystal Method: "High Roller"
Chap 2 - The Pogues: "The Sunnyside of the Street"
Chap 3 - DAG: "Supercollider"
Chap 4 - Fishbone: "Shakey Ground"
Chap 5 - Quarashi: "Stick Em Up"
Chap 6 - Pat Lundy: "City Of Stone"
Chap 7 - Wyclef Jean: "Sang Fezi"
Chap 8 - The Ting Tings: "Shut Up And Let Me Go"
Chap 9 - Fugazi: "Bad Mouth"
Chap 10 - Outkast: "Cruisin' In The ATL (Interlude)"
Chap 10 - Outkast: "Spaghetti Junction"
Chap 11 - Noot d' Noot: "Streetfighter"
Chap 12 - Beastie Boys: "So What'cha Want"
Chap 13 - Matisyahu: "Youth"
Chap 14 - Drivin-N-Cryin: "Straight To Hell"
Chap 15 - Renegade Soundwave: "Murder Music"
Chap 16 - Macy Gray: "The Letter"
Chap 17 - The Blind Boys Of Alabama: "No More"
Chap 18 - Jane's Addiction: "Mountain Song"

Chapter 1
DISCOVERY

The first time I broke the sound barrier, the accident was so startling that an image was seared into my mind: I was looking up from the ground, still seated in the chair that had toppled over; papers were floating in the air; my laptop was mid-flight, about to skitter across the floor; and globs of soda were frozen in space as they rained down from the ceiling.

CRACK!

The sound was the same as a whip's, only magnified a hundred times.

I lay there in stunned silence, ears ringing, long after the papers had fluttered to the ground. Coca-Cola was splattered all over the walls of the tiny break room.

It was after midnight. I had come into the office late to do an "urgent" repair on a computer for my boss. This job was a part-time, off-hours gig for me, and Tim had given me keys long ago so I could come and go as I pleased. On this particular night, I had decided to work in the break room so I could spread my books out on the empty table and study during down time.

It had taken me a couple of hours of wrestling with the disabled computer, but I'd finally gotten it working again. I'd filled out the paperwork and returned the computer to the shop. Then, as I gathered up my tools, I must have caused the can of Coke to explode somehow.

At least, that's what I initially thought—that the can had exploded.

But as I lay there on my back, my attention was drawn to a slow but steady drip coming from a joist in the ceiling. It was the remains of my soda can, embedded in a heavy wood beam that ran across the center of the room.

Embedded?

What could possibly have caused an explosion of such ferocity that it could launch my drink with that kind of force? The beam was splintered around a perfect circle, the bottom of the can still visible, two inches deep in the wood.

I was amazed at how much of a mess so little fluid could make. The can couldn't have been more than half full, but it had managed to cover everything in the room with a sticky brown mist: the table, the floor, my papers, the appliances, even the walls.

Standing up, I surveyed the tabletop, expecting burn marks or other damage. But other than the fact that everything had been misted with soda, there was no evidence of the violence that had just occurred. The heavy wooden table was a sticky mess, yet otherwise unharmed.

Soda continued to drip slowly from the beam, so I gathered a dishtowel from a drawer under the counter and placed it on the table. I removed another towel, dampened it in the sink, and began wiping down the cinderblock walls.

As I worked, I considered the source of the explosion. The room smelled like it always did, no hint of smoke. There was no source of fuel that could cause an explosion, like gunpowder or gasoline. I saw nothing on the table could have caused the explosion. There was very little even there: a closed plastic case containing a set of miniature screwdrivers for electronics; a small magnetic toy that people on break could fiddle with to make little sculptures; and my two textbooks, *New Venture Management* and *Corporate Strategy in a Global Economy*.

I had already put away the extension cord that I'd been using to run power to the computer I was working on. And I had put away the computer, eliminating the last possible source of any stored energy from—

My heart leaped into my throat as I remembered knocking my laptop off the table during the panic of the explosion.

Dear God, please tell me it still works!

I snatched it off the floor, placed it on the freshly wiped table, and carefully lifted the lid. An instant later it requested my password. A wave of relief washed over me—followed immediately by irritation. The upper right-hand corner of my LCD was cracked. Further inspection showed that the outer casing of the laptop was dented on that corner.

I typed in my password and ran a few tests. Other than a nasty black blotch in the corner of the screen, my computer worked just fine. I was annoyed at the damage, but overall realized that it could easily have been far worse. And I was overdue for a new system anyway; I'd just been waiting until after next month's graduation. I figured I'd have a real job soon enough; might as well wait until I could afford something nice.

My thoughts returned to the mystery. My computer had indeed been on the table. But clearly the laptop hadn't exploded. And it had been sitting a good eighteen inches away from the soda. Whatever had shot the can upward had to have been directly beneath it.

I continued cleaning, turning my attention to the floor. A thirty-page printout of a project I was working on had been sitting on the table next to my laptop. It was a formal business plan for a new company I had created for class. It was also the worst work I had ever churned out, so I was planning to gut it and start over as soon as I finished repairing that computer.

The pages had been scattered all over the floor. As I picked up the last of them, I found a multimeter buried underneath. I abruptly remembered precisely what it was I'd been doing at the exact instant the Coke can had left the table.

I'd been cleaning up, preparing to switch over to schoolwork. I had gathered up all the small screwdrivers, placed them back in the kit, and reached across the table to pick up the multimeter. I was pulling it toward myself so I could wind the leads around it and...

I was pretty sure I knew what had happened. Even though it made zero sense. One of the leads on the multimeter, I wasn't sure which, must have touched the can when I'd pulled it back across the table.

But where did the energy come from? Multimeters are simple devices that use next to no power. They don't store or deliver energy; they simply measure and monitor the electricity in other electrical devices—circuits, electrical components, wall outlets. There was no way that a little handheld multimeter could contain enough energy to cause such an explosion.

This particular multimeter was digital, and had a small nine-volt battery that powered the readout. I lifted it gingerly to examine it, taking great care to ensure that the two leads touched nothing. It was turned on and set to *Ohmmeter,* to measure resistance. The display read "000".

My brain struggled to wrap itself around the problem. I'd repaired the multimeter the previous week, but that hadn't been anything special. One of the techs had stepped on the unit, breaking the plastic case, and hadn't been able to get it to work again. It had taken me only a few minutes to find a loose wire, solder it back on, and tape the case back together. Voilà, good as new... if a bit redneckified for the duct tape.

Since then, the other techs had been using it without complaint. I had used it several times myself with no problem. So how the hell had it blown up my can of Coke?

It was then that I decided to try replicating the event.

I grabbed a fresh can of Coke out of the company fridge, and was about to grab the multimeter, when I thought of safety. Leaving the multimeter untouched on the table, I went out into the shop to gather up safety goggles and earplugs. I took these items, plus the can of Coke, outside behind the building. I made a separate trip for the multimeter so I could be sure it touched nothing.

Standing outside in the dead of night, I surveyed the small fleet of service vans. It still amazed me whenever I saw them all together, lined up like that. Tim had turned this little venture into a robust business. It had been pretty impressive to watch it happen, and I was proud to have been a part of it, even if I'd mostly been along for the ride.

Tim Carithers had started this business in his garage five years ago and had quickly turned a profit. I was his very first employee—hired on as an assistant. It was a great fit for me. I've always had a knack for all things electronic. As a kid, I would regularly scrape together every penny I could to buy RC car and plane kits.

I was a senior in high school when Tim hired me. I was looking for a straight way to make some money and he was willing to take a chance on a kid he knew nothing about. For the first few months I did little more than hand him tools and watch him work, but he was a good teacher, and I was an eager student. I picked up on computer repair quickly. As the business grew, he began diagnosing simple repairs and then handing them over to me. It wasn't long before he trusted me to both diagnose *and* repair with very little supervision.

Tim had no family and I had no father. I suppose we filled those voids for each other. When my mom passed away right before I graduated high school, Tim even offered to take me in. But I was eighteen and ready to get out on my own.

I'd spent my high school years as a 'B' student, mostly due to lack of interest, but had tested very well. My SATs were high enough to get me into the elite Goizueta School of Business at Emory University. Still, Emory is a very expensive private institution and I would never have been able to afford it, had there not been a special program available to employees. My mother had put in twenty years of mopping floors and wiping tables.

So after graduation, I sold my mom's house and moved into a little apartment near campus. I continued working with Tim on a part-time basis while I was in school.

Tim's business flourished, and eventually it outgrew his garage. After an extended search, Tim finally decided to buy an abandoned firehouse on the north side of Atlanta, in an industrial section of Doraville—right down the road from where I grew up. I spent the summer of my freshman year hanging sheetrock, painting, and otherwise restoring the old cinderblock building. When it was done, Tim reinvented the marketing of his company, renaming it *911 Computer Services*, inspired by the old firehouse location.

Now I looked at one of the clearest signs of Tim's success: six service vans bathed in the light of a full moon. And for better or worse, Tim was as corny as he was brilliant; each of the vans had been done up like an ambulance. Tim had even gone so far as to raid Big Jim's Salvage Yard for real (but non-working) ambulance lights.

A distant dog sang to the moon as I cautiously peered about the gravel lot. My nervousness was unwarranted. The lot was surrounded by a ten-foot fence, which was topped with a spool of razor-sharp barbed wire. It was a tough area, and the insurance underwriter had insisted on serious security measures.

16

I was all alone as I spread out the components of my little experiment on a picnic bench near the back door. The can of soda sat in the middle of the table. I carefully laid the multimeter on one side of the table, then took the positive lead and walked it over to the opposite side. The lead was attached to the multimeter by a twenty-four-inch red wire, and the can was now roughly at its middle point.

Satisfied, I put on the goggles and pushed in the earplugs. Squatting down beside the multimeter so that most of my body was below the table, I slowly pulled the red wire toward me. Slowly, slowly, slowly, and then…

Nothing.

The lead had touched the can, clear as day. I stood up, grasped the positive lead in my hand like a pencil, and boldly poked the can.

Still nothing.

It must have been the negative lead that had sparked the explosion. So I laid my experiment out again, only this time using the black wire. I squatted down once again and slowly began to draw the wire toward myself.

Again, nothing.

Damn. I was sure that was going to work. I poked the can with the negative lead, to no avail. Maybe both leads had to touch it?

I picked up the can and sat it back down on top of the negative lead, pinning its tip to the wooden table. I was even more cautious than before as I draped the positive lead across the table—I was pretty confident this was going to work. Crouching down again, I cringed with anticipation as I began slowly pulling the red wire toward me.

Nothing.

Nothing? What could be different? The only obvious difference from before was that this time I'd intentionally left the can unopened, not wanting to get sprayed again. So I popped the top, dumped half of the contents into the bush, and then repeated the series of experiments again.

Still nothing! It was almost three a.m., and I was tired and extremely frustrated.

Looking back on it now, I wish to hell I had just surrendered at that moment. I could have gone in and crashed on the couch in Tim's office. Life would have gone on its merry way, and so many horrible things would never have happened. And someday, somewhere, somebody *else* would have made this discovery. Anybody but me.

Unfortunately, I remembered the magnetic toy sitting on the break room table.

A few minutes later, I had the first experiment set up again—with the can in the middle of the table and the red lead draped across it. Only this time I was going to drag the wire over the magnetic toy as I bumped the can. I eyed the now open and half-empty can and briefly considered going in for an unopened soda, but that seemed like too much trouble. Slowly I pulled the wire across the table.

SMASH!

I was covered in soda once again. Shit.

The can had not shot up into the sky. Instead, it had collapsed onto itself, slammed straight through the table—splintering a gaping hole in the wooden surface—and buried itself into the earth below. And, of course, it had once again sprayed sticky soda all over me with the force of a compressor-driven power spray.

I was both annoyed and elated.

I had peeled my shirt off and was holding my head under the faucet in the break room sink when I had a realization. The can going down into the dirt was the exact opposite of what I had expected to happen. And I'd touched the can with the positive lead. So what if I used the negative lead?

A moment later I was back outside with wet hair, no shirt,

and a fresh can of soda. I lay my experiment out, only this time with the negative lead and an *empty* can of soda. And I had to move down the table a bit, to avoid the damaged section.

BOOM!

Despite the earplugs, the noise was extremely loud. My whole body felt the concussion of the blast: a sudden escape and return of the air around me.

I had been staring right at the can with deep concentration, yet I wasn't sure what had happened. The can was simply gone. It seemed to have just disappeared into thin air. It was there, then not.

I rushed back inside and returned with the half-empty twelve-pack. This time I decided not to open the can. If it exploded, then at least the evidence would be painted all over my body, even if it happened too fast for me to see. Besides, another dousing would be par for the course.

But the result was just as confounding: a deep boom, a concussion, and a disappearing Coke can—but no spray.

So… no explosion, per se, just a super-loud bang and a disappearing can. I felt fairly sure the full can must have stayed intact, though, which meant the cans were traveling upward at a faster rate than my eyes could track.

Of course, there was no way for me to guess that I was launching cans of soda out of Earth's atmosphere at nearly three times the speed of sound.

It wasn't long before it occurred to me to try changing the settings on the multimeter. It was set to two million ohms, so I dialed it way back twenty thousand. And this time, when the negative lead hit the can, it shot off at high velocity… but no BOOM. And unlike the previous launches, I actually heard the can hit the roof of a nearby warehouse as it returned to earth.

I gulped down the last warm sip of my final Coke can,

dialed the multi down to two thousand, and hit the empty container with the negative lead. The can flung itself straight up into the air at about the same speed at which I could throw it, peaked at about forty feet, then clattered to the ground right in front of me.

The lowest setting on the multi was two hundred ohms, so I tried it. When the lead touched the can, it popped up a few inches and fell over. I tried it a few more times with the same result.

At this low setting, nothing was exploding or shooting off violently. The event seemed so innocuous, in fact, that I even worked up the nerve to steady the can with one hand while I touched it with the negative lead.

I felt no shock, nothing: just the can pushing upward. When my palm was above it, the can would push my hand up about six inches. In fact, it insisted upon rising up off the table. If I pushed back down, the can crumpled—and refused to be pushed any lower than about six inches above the table.

It was then that I discovered that, if I continued to touch the can with the negative lead, the can would levitate indefinitely.

Chapter 2
PRESENTATION

I'm convinced that my mother's heart was holding out for my acceptance to Emory. Going into my final high school semester, I had graduation in the bag and acceptance letters from all three of my backup schools, but no word yet from Emory.

Emory is world renowned for its schools of Medicine and Law, but the School of Business quietly competes at a very elite level with far less fanfare. Though my SAT score put me in the top 99.9% of those who took the test, my grades were average at best, and I hadn't participated in any school-sponsored team sports or any of the other stuff, like volunteer work, that college-bound kids did to pad their applications. I figured I was doing well just to stay out of jail.

So knowing how elite the school's business department was, I never got my hopes up. But Mom seemed to believe it was my destiny, so I applied. Having little else to point to, I focused my application letter on the fact that I had taken a Silver Glove when I was fifteen, and a Golden Glove the following year.

Despite my pessimism, two days before midterms I received an invitation to join Emory University's Boxing Club. The next afternoon I arrived home to find my mom holding my acceptance letter, tears of joy rolling down her cheeks.

And the following morning I found her lifeless body crumpled on the kitchen floor.

I arrived at Emory with a spiritual directive: I was on a mission to live the life that my mom had envisioned for me.

At times like these—huddled in a hallway with a bunch of nervous, sweaty over-achievers—I wondered if this was precisely what she had in mind.

Professor Treadwell—or "Tom" as he preferred to be called—had scheduled New Venture business plans to be presented over three marathon days, ten presentations each day. We were each expected to present our business plan in ten minutes, which would then be followed by a five-minute Q&A session. This was the first day, and ten of us sat in the hall, waiting to be called in.

Greg nudged me. "Check out Kermit." I looked up, and he nodded down the hall.

Jessica was smiling broadly at the wall in front of her, her lips moving ever so slightly like a crazy lady at a bus stop, clearly practicing a speech in her head. I shared a nervous chuckle with Greg.

Every class has one. Jessica was the first to put her hand in the air the moment a professor stopped speaking; was frequently spotted coming out of a teacher's office; automatically volunteered for any kiss-ass endeavor; and would probably melt down completely if she ever received a B.

She was very tightly wound, and somewhere along the line somebody had pointed out that her ass was probably as water tight as a frog's butt. Thus the nickname Kermit was born.

When it came time to schedule the presentations, Jessica, as usual, had volunteered to go first. Then, when no one else volunteered, Treadwell said the rest of us would go in alphabetical order.

Lord, I hate that.

With a name like Dale Adams, you get used to going first whenever teachers "randomly" decide to go in alphabetical order. I'd been putting up with that for my whole life. So thank God for Kiss-Ass Kermy or I'd be going first yet again. I was still second, but hey, small victories.

As I watched Jessica rehearsing her speech, a large, white-haired man in a suit came lumbering down the hallway pulling a briefcase on wheels. He passed through the middle of us without even acknowledging our existence, and when he stopped at the door to the conference room, I had a sudden thrill of nervousness. His late arrival must account for why nobody had been called in yet... so maybe the stay of execution was over.

The nervous chatter ended as everyone else in the hall realized the same thing.

Suddenly I was acutely aware of how much I hated wearing suits. The collar chafed my neck, my pants felt bunched up on my crotch, I was hotter than hell, and the jacket was driving me crazy.

But this was the life I had chosen. If professional baseball players could be comfortable in tight pants, then surely I could come to terms with business attire.

Finally the door to the conference room opened, and Mr. Treadwell popped out. "Ms. Osgood?"

"Yes, Tom?" came the cheery answer from down the hall. Jessica stood up quickly and made her way forward without waiting for an answer.

"I don't envy you having to go after Kermit," commented Greg. "I'd rather be the only non-Asian in a calculus class."

I couldn't help cracking up. "Yeah, well..."

Treadwell ignored the other students in the hall as he ushered Jessica in. He was a tall, thinly built man, and wore dark slacks and a white suit shirt, but no tie. The disheveled hair, too-long goatee, and casually undone top buttons on his shirt told the world that he had earned the right to take leave of corporate norms. He had no one to impress. This was further proof of Treadwell's mantra: "I ain't some ivory tower professor."

And it was true. The guy was a rock star in the business world. He had a weekly column in the *Atlanta Business Chronicle*, had written three books, and his op-ed pieces frequently showed up in the *Wall Street Journal* and *New York Times*. He was a regular guest commentator on *Money Line* and other news programs. Twice he left our class early because he was due across town at CNN's studios.

Competition had been fierce when it was announced that he was teaching one MBA and one undergrad class, with only thirty slots available in each. The undergrad class had been limited to graduating seniors, and within that group all interested names went into a lottery. I was elated to get in. Not only was I a graduating senior, but this would be my very last class. Talk about going out with a bang.

From the beginning, Treadwell had told us he had no interest in attendance—if we didn't show up, it was our loss. He didn't care about grades, either. On the first day of class, he told us, "You're all getting an 'A' in this class. Merry Christmas."

There would be two tests, a midterm and a final. All we really had to do was sign our names to them. "Yes, I will still grade the tests," he pointed out, "but that will only be to satisfy my curiosity."

The only work we had to do was come up with a business idea, support it in a detailed formal business plan, then present it to real investors.

This presentation was truly a testament to the epic magnitude of getting into Thomas Treadwell's class. This exercise was pointedly *not* some theoretical simulation dreamed up by an academic with no real-world experience. We were presenting our ideas to *real* venture capitalists and angel investors.

Suddenly the conference room door swung open, and Jessica burst through. I glanced at my watch: twelve minutes exactly. What the...?

Jessica stormed past, nose in the air, tears streaming down her face, right down the middle of the hall without so much as a glance left or right.

Treadwell's words came back to me: "These guys aren't coming here for the fun of it. I told them you're the very best Emory has to offer. One of you is going to give them their next big venture. They're coming because they want to make *money*. This is the real thing. If you come in with a half-assed idea that you aren't prepared to defend, they *will* rip you to shreds."

Statistically speaking, just getting a raw idea in front of a group of serious venture capitalists is pretty rare. Rarer still is one of those raw ideas actually getting backing and being brought to fruition through VC. Sure, someone might fail to get VC attention, go off and scrounge up a bit of capital, put things in motion on their own, and *then*—once some promise is on the table—*maybe* bring in VC at a later stage. But a VC almost never wastes their time on a raw, unproven idea.

"During a pitch to investors," Treadwell had said, "there are two forces at work. First, the VCs want to make money: they want ideas worthy of investment. Second, and more important, the VCs *do not* want to lose money. You guys will be given precisely ten minutes to make your case, and precisely five minutes to defend it during a vigorous discussion. And that's only if you're pitch is worthy of conversation. Your job will be to convince some very cagey people into *giving you money*, so come prepared or you will embarrass yourself. And me."

As I watched Jessica's figure retreating down the hall, Treadwell's warnings became very, very real.

Turning back, I found all eyes on me, wide with fear. Treadwell had used the word "vigorous" to describe the Q&A, but...

Oh God.

After what seemed like a million years, the door opened again. "Mr. Adams?"

Oh God.

Now I questioned the wisdom of coming in here with a less-than-half-baked idea. I had dropped my original business plan two weeks earlier, the same night that my can of Coke exploded, and rushed to build a new plan. Then, a mere two nights ago, I'd scrapped that plan, too, and started over. Two days' prep time. Two months wouldn't have been enough.

Oh God.

I mustered what courage I could, stood up, and made my way in, lugging a duffel bag with me. The room was long and narrow, with a large, shiny oak table in the center. There was a computer off to the side nearest the door and a large screen on the wall. On the screen was a PowerPoint slide reading "Questions & Answers."

Jessica left her presentation on the computer? Wow. The queen of composure must have been completely dismantled by the end of her presentation.

Mr. Treadwell took his seat at the end of the table, directly facing the screen, and I walked over to the computer. My hands shook as I removed Jessica's thumb drive and replaced it with mine.

It took me a few moments to queue up my PowerPoint presentation. All the while, silence. No chitchat. No recap of Jessica's presentation. No nothing. Just silence.

I looked up. The guy closest to me had been watching

me intently... but suddenly he yawned and looked away. Seven bored faces, no emotion. One was slouched in his chair, tapping his pen on the table, staring at the ceiling. Another shuffled through some papers in front of him. No communication. In fact, no one was looking directly at anybody, except for Treadwell, who was watching me with a patient half smile.

There was no emotion here whatsoever. Not even a hint of residue left from whatever drama had brought Jessica to tears.

What was it that felt so familiar?

"Mr. Adams, we don't have all day," came the uncharacteristically stern admonishment from Treadwell.

I knew exactly what this was. I was at a beer-soaked game of poker in a frat house. The stakes had gone uncomfortably high because they all had good hands. But they were trying to act like they didn't care. These guys were old chums. They were planning to chew me up and spit me out. The only thing missing was cigar smoke.

Shit.

I reached into my bag and pulled out seven information packages, each containing a copy of all my PowerPoint slides and a thirty-page formal business plan. I walked around and distributed these packages. I glanced at my watch, queued up my first slide with a tiny remote, and turned to face the firing squad.

The slide featured a floating astronaut and proclaimed:

No G Enterprises
presents
The Future of Everything

"Good morning, gentlemen," I said loudly, smiling at the expectant faces around the table in an attempt to project confidence. No one was fooled. "No G Enterprises is an electronics manufacturer dedicated to revolutionizing the world by exploring and developing products that defy gravity."

I glanced around at the uninterested faces and clicked to the next slide, which showed an old Powell Peralta skateboard along with some skateboard industry statistics. I continued: "As you can see, there are more than eleven million skateboard enthusiasts in the US, and that gives us a domestic market worth more than $4.8 billion dollars last year."

At this point I could tell there was a bit of vague interest. I took a deep breath and plunged ahead. "We are going to build a skateboard that every single skater on the planet *must* have."

I clicked to the next slide. It showed the same skateboard, only now the wheels had big red X's over them. "What if you could get rid of the wheels entirely—and make a skate board that could float on air?"

I paused dramatically and pulled up my next slide. "Introducing the ZG Board. 'ZG' stands for 'zero gravity,' of course. It is my belief that not only will every existing skater buy—"

"Oh, I get it. Like the one Michael J. Fox used in *Back to the Future*?"

I completely missed the sarcasm.

"Yes, exactly!" I smiled and pointed at the speaker. It was Michael Simons, chairman of the board for the Greener Georgia Project, a conservation group that funded energy-efficient initiatives. Treadwell had given us dossiers on every member of his panel so that we could tailor our presentations accordingly.

Feeling pleased that I was getting through, I continued. "I think the ZG will spark a fad, bringing out old and young alike to try…"

I trailed off as I watched Simons stand and gather up the

report I had given him. As he walked to the door, he turned to Treadwell. "I'm going to take a piss. I trust you'll get rid of this pathetic product of our public education system before I return."

Simons dropped my papers in the trash as he stepped through the door. I was completely stunned. I'm sure my mouth was hanging wide open. Then Keith Evans—the franchise king, owner of more than fifty McDonald's restaurants, ten stores in a retail chain, a jazz club in Buckhead, and various other businesses—began to cackle.

Treadwell groaned.

"Maybe it was a mistake to tell them I was giving out A's automatically," Treadwell said, shaking his head irritably. The cackle broke into outright laughter, and now Evans's mirth was shared by two more panelists. Treadwell's expression was angrier than I had ever seen it. "Dale, I liked you. What a shame. I've got half a mind to eject you from my class after this cute little stunt. You need to get out of here right now. Don't talk to anyone in the hall: just go."

"But—"

"You've been *DISMISSED!*" Treadwell practically shouted. Clearly his patience was gone. The panel believed my presentation was some kind of adolescent fraternity prank, and Simons felt deeply insulted. Treadwell needed to control the damage.

"Oh come on, Tom," said Evans, trying to overcome his laughter. "You've got to admit it was funny. We were just about to screw with him, but he screwed with us first! The ZG? Funny stuff, kid. You've got serious balls, pulling a prank on this crowd! Huevos *grandes*. ¡Muy grande, amigo!"

As he spoke, I dug around in my bag.

"Don't be a poor sport, Tom," agreed Cynthia McKinzie, former Ma Bell exec, philanthropist, and angel investor. She specialized in tech startups. "After what we just did to that first girl, we had it coming. It's just a joke."

"It's not a joke," I said quietly. I gently laid a skateboard on the table. It was a blank with no wheels. I had glued aluminum foil to the underside and mounted a little wooden box off to the side.

McKinzie raised her brows at me, as if to warn me not to push my luck. Evans was smiling widely with an expectation of hilarity. I could tell it wouldn't take much to push him over the edge. This was the hand I was dealt, so I figured I might as well play it out.

I picked up the board and pretended to listen to the black box. Pursing my lips together, I blew out a long, steady stream of breath: "Ptptptptptptptptpt!"

I zoomed around the room with the board over my head, pretending it was flying. Evans laughed so hard I thought he was going to pass out. Everyone was cracking up. Even Treadwell couldn't help himself.

Rounding the table after a second lap, I stopped behind Treadwell and placed the board on the table right in front of him. "Mr. Treadwell, would you please press the button?"

"No, I don't think so," he replied, pushing the suspicious device to the middle of the table.

"I'm game," Evans asserted without missing a beat. He leaned in and pressed the red button I had mounted on top of the black box.

Instantly, all laughter ceased.

The board was floating exactly six inches above the table. Everyone was mesmerized. Nobody even noticed me as I walked back to the head of the table.

Miles Prestone, head of the Pylotica Economic Studies think tank and founder of a multinational consulting firm, was the first to find words. They came out as practically a whisper. "Wow. Now *that* is really cool."

"Yes," I answered. "But probably not the best use of the

technology. If you guys look at the report I gave you, you'll see a couple of pages devoted to bigger things." No one was listening. Evans had reached out and tried to pass his hand under the board. It glided away from him. "Well, I hope you guys will take some time to read the report later."

I leaned over and pushed the board back to Evans. "You have to put a hand on top to steady it before you put anything underneath."

Evans did as I'd suggested, steadying the board from above with one hand, and putting his other hand underneath. The board levitated six inches above his lower hand. "It's focused on your hand now, so you can take your other hand off the top."

He did, then raised his lower hand upward slowly. The board moved with it, maintaining a six-inch gap.

"You think that's cool, check this out," I said, taking the board from Evans and placing it on the floor. I stepped onto it, and with one kick, glided around the room, leaning to turn and riding it exactly as one would a skateboard with wheels.

"Mr. Evans, could you come put your hand under the board again, then try lifting?" I asked, stopping at the front of the room.

Evans rose without a word and walked to the front. He kneeled down and ran his hand under the center of the board and lifted. I don't think he realized how easy this would be; he almost knocked me off the board. I bent at the knees to steady myself as he slowly rose to his feet. When he was fully standing, he extended his hand straight out in front of himself, at chest level. The board, with me on top of it, continued to hover six inches above his hand.

"Gentlemen, I'm six feet tall and weigh a hundred and eighty pounds," I said. I looked around and let this fact sink in. It was clear to my audience that Evans wasn't exerting himself in the slightest as he held me in midair. "Mr. Evans, would you be so kind as to quickly withdraw your hand and drop me to the floor?"

Evans turned to the side, fast enough that I almost lost my balance. He waited until I steadied myself, then yanked his hand back. I floated gently downward, coming to a stop six inches from the floor, right in front of Simons. I hadn't noticed his return.

"Mr. Simons," I said, clearing my throat. "I'm very sorry to have offended you earlier. But I assure you there was no malice intended, and—as you can plainly see—I was not pulling a prank."

Simons just stood there. He was obviously at a loss for words, so I casually fished my report out of the trash and handed it to him. He took the papers numbly and returned to his seat.

I glanced at my watch, then picked up the board and put it back on the table, letting it hover tantalizingly.

"Unfortunately," I said, looking up at the screen as I clicked forward through my additional slides. "This hasn't gone the way it was supposed to, and I'm pretty much out of time, so we might as well skip ahead to the Q&A."

I stopped at the final slide. It read plainly: Questions & Answers.

"Does anyone have any questions?"

Before I even finished speaking, Treadwell blurted out: "How? How does it work, and how is it powered? And what... why... what the hell is this, Dale?"

"To be frank, I'm still working on the why. I am clearer on the how, but even that needs further study. What I *am* sure of is that I'm able to communicate two bits of information to objects at a molecular level. I can tell an object to either 'attract' or to 'repulse.' I made this skateboard float by telling the aluminum underneath to 'repulse.'"

I wasn't sure if this made any sense; it didn't make a whole ton of sense to me either, to be honest. So I plowed ahead. "In addition, I can control the volume of my command. Right now I'm telling this skateboard to 'repulse' at barely a whisper. If I crank up the volume and 'yell,' so to speak, the board would shoot upward through the ceiling so quickly it would almost seem to disappear."

The board was slowly gliding toward me, so I reached out and steadied it as I opened the black box. I was young, but I had no interest in being anybody's fool: I had taken steps to obfuscate the simplicity of my device. The multimeter had been disguised by pulling the guts out of the plastic housing and putting them into the little wooden box—so when you looked into the box, it just looked like a jumble of wires and electronics. But even if somebody figured out that it was just a plain ole multi, the truth was still two huge steps away: a magnet hidden in the bottom of the box and the extra drip of solder.

That last would be pretty hard to catch. As it turns out, after the tech had stepped on the multimeter weeks earlier, I had indeed screwed up the repair job. While soldering the loose wire back on, I'd apparently allowed an extra bit of solder to drip down. This had connected two points that should not have been connected.

Leaving the box open for all to see, I pushed the board back toward Treadwell. "As you can see, this is nothing fancy—about fifteen dollars' worth of electronics."

"*This* is all the power it needs?" asked an incredulous Treadwell, holding up a wire with a single nine-volt battery dangling from it. "This is all it takes to lift a one-hundred-eighty-pound man?"

I smiled. "Crazy, isn't it? But when I sell it, it will come with a battery that lasts forever."

They had all been examining the contents of the black box, but now every head swiveled in my direction. I was a little surprised that everyone caught the implications instantly. And I was glad Simons had decided to return; he was the panelist I felt would be the most interested in my other ideas.

"My original plan was to pitch an everlasting battery to you guys, using the same principles as the skateboard. Have you ever seen one of those flashlights that you charge up just by shaking it?" I looked around the room. "The way a shake light works is that it has a hollow copper coil with a small magnet inside. As you shake, the magnet slides back and forth, and the magnetic field traveling through the coil creates a little pulse of electricity. I took those principles and created a simple circuit that turns on when the magnet is at the bottom of the coil. When that circuit turns on, the magnet is repelled up through the tube. And then, as soon as the weight of the magnet is lifted, the circuit switches off and the magnet drops back down—which turns the circuit back on, and the whole process repeats indefinitely." I looked around; it was clear that they were following along. "Basically, I managed to create a permanent cycle—a shake light that shakes itself forever."

"But this is Emory, not Georgia Tech," I said. "I know just enough about electronics to get into trouble, but I'm not an engineer. A normal shake light uses a simple capacitor to store energy: you shake it a few times, and the stored energy powers the light for a minute or two. But with my device... well, after a half hour or so, it had generated so much energy that it overwhelmed the capacitor, and the whole thing literally melted down." I smiled ruefully. "But it should be pretty simple to create an inexpensive sensor that would switch power generation on and off automatically as needed. That could be a whole other product line. Imagine batteries that could run an entire household forever, with no monthly bills."

The entire panel seemed to be frozen in place. No one

said a word. They just stared at me as if I were an alien.

"Well, look, you guys have spent twenty minutes with me," I said casually, closing the black box and packing up. I needed to leave them hungry. "My contact information is in the package I gave you. Please feel free to use it."

"Mr. Adams!"

My hand was on the doorknob when Treadwell spoke. I turned back. "Yes, sir?"

"When you come to school Monday, would you please come prepared for a longer conversation after class?"

I wanted to spike the ball and do an obnoxious victory dance, but I answered with reserve: "Yes, sir."

"And one more thing," said Treadwell. He stood up and made his way toward me. "Would you do me a favor and wipe that smile off your face before you go out there? And leave quickly. Don't say a word to anybody."

I smiled, then quickly un-smiled. "Yes, sir."

Chapter 3
TROUBLE

Monday morning found me running behind schedule. I hate walking into class late. When I arrived, Mr. Treadwell's classroom door was wide open but he was nowhere in sight. There were four smartly dressed people sitting in the front row, and another leaning against the desk facing the class. I recognized one as my academic counselor.

The lady leaning against the desk smiled warmly. "You're in the right place. Come on in, it's okay."

Everyone was quiet as I lugged my duffel bag up the steps and grabbed a seat next to Greg. I looked around; everyone seemed to be waiting for something. "What's up?" I asked Greg.

"Heck if I know," he shrugged. "Guess Treadwell's running late."

"How'd your speech go?" I asked.

"Dude," he said, shaking his head. "Those guys were assholes. They didn't have to be like that. One of them said my business idea was stupid. Can you believe that? He literally called it 'stupid.' To my face. Man, fuck them."

That must have been rough. I bet no one had called him "stupid" since he was in grade school. Greg was a very likeable, happy-go-lucky kind of guy: eternally smiling, quick with a joke, always with a different girl for each arm. I can't imagine somebody finding something they disliked enough about him to call him "stupid."

"How did *your* presentation go?" he asked.

"Mine went well, I guess." I didn't want to make him feel bad, so I didn't elaborate. "The beginning was rough, but then things smoothed out. And nobody called me stupid. What the hell did you say, dumb-ass?"

"Bite me." Greg laughed. "What's up with the suit, man? You got an interview after class or something?"

The lady at the front closed the door and cleared her throat for attention. I breathed a sigh of relief.

"It's about a quarter after, and pretty much everyone is here. I would like to call roll." She held up a clipboard and began reading. "Dale Adams?"

"Here," I answered. Roll call? Really?

When she finished, she asked each of the four strangers on the front row to stand up as she introduced them by name.

"…and my name is Jill Henson," she concluded. "We are all counselors here at Emory. Many of you know us well. But what you might *not* know is that each of us has had training and experience in helping people deal with grief." No pause to let that sink in. "Unfortunately, I have some very bad news for you. Your professor, Thomas Treadwell, passed away yesterday afternoon."

Just like that. There were several gasps around the room. I couldn't believe it.

"If you would, please take a moment and jot down the information on the board." She stepped to the side and gestured at the contact information for herself and the other four counselors written on the markerboard. "I want you guys to know that we are all available for you twenty-four hours a day for as long as it takes to help you work through this. We—"

"What happened?" interrupted Greg. "We all saw him last week. He seemed fine."

She answered slowly. "That's right, he was fine. This was just a very unfortunate accident. The cause is still being looked into, but it appears he died from carbon monoxide poisoning, due to a faulty A/C unit." She paused. "His wife perished in the same accident."

Now there were several people sobbing in the room. I felt numb. I didn't really know the guy, but I liked him. His class was ultra-informal, lots of discussion and going back and forth. Greg and some of the guys had run into him in the Highlands once, and drank all night with him. He was a celebrity, yes, but he was a very genuine, sincerely nice guy.

"I know that it's very difficult to think of things like this at the moment, but there are a few matters of practicality that I must address." Jill Henson cleared her throat. "I have pulled your files, and I'm aware that you are all seniors set to graduate in a few weeks. It goes without saying that this class is over and you will all get full credit for completing it. We will be…"

She continued talking for a while, but I didn't pay much attention. None of it really mattered. And I felt guilty, because I knew a terrible tragedy had occurred, and yet I couldn't help but think of how it had inconvenienced *me*. I had come to class today loaded for bear. I was going to give the speech of a lifetime to a group of very interested investors. What the hell was I supposed to do now?

I struggled to overcome my inappropriate disappointment. I tried to focus on Treadwell.

What a shame. He really was a super-cool guy.

After Ms. Henson finished talking about the "practicalities," and reminded us once again that the counselors were all there for us, to help us work through our grief, we were dismissed.

Most of us wandered out to the quad, where we sat making small talk, telling stories about Treadwell, talking about how crazy this whole thing was. There was a lot of crying, which drew attention in the busy courtyard. Someone suggested we all meet back there that evening for an impromptu memorial service. Someone else suggested we invite the students in the other New Venture Management class Treadwell had been teaching. Jessica volunteered to go get a list of phone numbers from the counselors.

With a plan in place, I decided to go home and come back later. On my way, I popped in to a gas station to pick up a pack of cigarettes. I had quit fourteen months earlier, but suddenly felt the need for the comfort of my oldest friend. Excuses, excuses.

I was pretty distracted, still trying to think my way through the news of Treadwell's death, but luckily I did see the dog just in time. I was coming out of a fairly steep curve on Ponce De Leon when a little white mutt darted in front my '93 Celica. I slammed on the brakes and went into a screeching slide. In my rearview mirror I could see the driver of a black sedan also jamming on his brakes.

Even as I breathed a sigh of relief that I hadn't been rear-ended, something in my peripheral vision caused me to glance to the right at the very last second. I saw a dump truck running the stop sign. Abruptly the entire world went sideways. I found myself spinning round and round wildly. My car came to a sudden halt.

I sat there for what seemed like an hour in stunned silence. The passenger side of the car was pushed closer to me by about a foot. I smelled dirt, grass, and something unnatural. Oil mixed with antifreeze? I heard the hiss of steam escaping. My windshield was completely crushed, but I could see the shadow of a crumpled hood.

"You all right, buddy?"

The passenger window had been rolled up, but now it was gone altogether. That explained the glass all over me.

"I think so," I said, glancing down. There was blood all over my white shirt and tie. "Shit! Can you give me a hand getting—?"

The man was already gone. I saw him walk toward a group of people and gesture back at me, but he didn't break stride. As the others began making their way over, the man headed toward the black sedan that had been behind me.

I wiggled my fingers. Check. I wiggled my toes. Check. I wanted to see where the blood was coming from, but the rearview mirror was gone.

Then people were all over the place.

"It's okay, just hold on buddy! Help is on the way!"

"Can you move your fingers? What's your name? Don't fall asleep."

"Can I call someone for you?"

I undid my seatbelt and tried the door. It wouldn't budge.

"Please don't move. I know you want to get out, but please wait until help arrives."

I lifted one leg. Wiggled it a bit. Then I did the same to the other leg. Seemed okay. I visually inspected and wiggled both my arms. Everything seemed functional, so I decided to get the hell out of what was left of my car.

I threw my shoulder into the door with force. Still nothing, except more urgings to sit still and wait. I climbed toward the passenger door, which was halfway crushed in, and pulled the handle while pushing the door.

"Can you get this door open?" I asked a big guy who was standing behind the man who kept urging me to sit still. Without answering he came forward, grabbed the door, and started pulling. I pushed with him. Another guy came forward to help him, but no luck.

"Ain't gonna happen, friend," said the big guy.

They helped me climb out the window. I gingerly walked around, then hopped a bit, and cautiously spun my arms like a windmill. "I think I'm okay."

I gave what must have been a pretty unsightly, bloody grin.

"You're one lucky guy. I saw the whole thing. If that dog hadn't run out into the road…"

"Where's the guy in the truck? Is he okay?" I asked.

"He ran off, must've been drunk. There's beer cans all over the place."

I surveyed my car. The front passenger-side wheel was buckled out and horizontal to the ground. The engine compartment had taken the brunt of the impact and was completely demolished. It looked like a bomb had blown away half the engine.

I heard sirens in the distance, getting ever closer.

Walking around to the driver's side, I could see that the car was dug into the ground. The front wheel on this side had also buckled, and had disappeared almost entirely beneath the car.

If I had arrived at that intersection just a split second earlier, that dump truck would have T-boned me. Flat out. I'd be dead as a doorknob were it not for that dog.

Someone was coming toward me with a wet towel. I guessed it was the owner of the house whose grass my car had just tore all to hell. "Here. For your face."

I began gently wiping my face, carefully in case there were any bits of broken glass. Police officers were approaching on foot. Pretty soon the paramedics were there. It seemed to me like a lifetime had passed, but all of it—from the instant the truck hit me till the moment the police arrived—had probably taken less than five minutes.

I sat in the back of an ambulance while a paramedic poked and prodded and a police officer took my statement.

"Looks like a pretty simple case of drunk driving and fleeing the scene," concluded the officer. "We'll track this guy down, then you'll probably have to come to court."

"No problem, officer."

"Can we go ahead and take him to the hospital now?" asked the paramedic.

"Yeah, go ahead."

"Wait! I don't want to go the hospital. I don't have health insurance."

"You have insurance on your car," said the officer, holding up his accident report. "That should cover you. And since I'm assigning the blame to our missing truck driver, it's actually his insurance that'll cover you."

"Listen, I feel fine and I just don't want to go." I hopped up and danced a jig to demonstrate the point.

"No, *you* listen," admonished the EMT. "You've got a bloody nose that may or may not be broken, and a nasty knock to the head that tells me there's a good chance you've suffered a concussion. The doctor will want to keep you overnight."

Hell, no.

I reached up and felt my nose tenderly. It smarted fiercely, but wasn't broken. "Believe me, my nose is not broken. It's been broken twice, so I know exactly what that feels like. And I've had concussions on more than one occasion. So I know what that feels like, too."

I enjoy boxing, but it has its drawbacks. No matter how fast you are, given time you'll take some good shots.

"Believe me, I do *not* have a concussion." I looked at the officer. "He can't *make* me go with him, can he?"

"Well, I agree with him that you should go. Concussions are nothing to take lightly. And it can't hurt to get checked out." He sighed. "But no, he can't force you to go with him."

"I know you're just doing your job," I told the paramedic. "But I think I'm going to pass on a trip to the hospital. If I feel weird or whatever, I promise to go straight the ER. I live right down the street from DeKalb Memorial."

I turned to the policeman. "Can I get my stuff out of the car before the tow truck gets here?"

"Sure. Can I call somebody for you?"

"I have a cell phone. I'll call my boss to come get me."

Where the hell was my phone? It should have been in the center console of the Celica.

I eventually found it under the driver's seat. Damn it— the screen was cracked. Despite the bulky fifty-dollar case that was supposed to protect it. It still worked, though.

I finished gathering all my stuff from the car, then called the office. "Tim left a while ago. You should try him on his cell."

That was good; maybe that meant he was closer to this side of town. But when I tried his cell, I got sent straight to voice mail. So I hung up and decided to call Greg. "Dude. You're never going to believe this."

Greg arrived just in time to get a good look at my car on the back of the tow truck before it pulled away. He was duly impressed.

On the way to my place, we stopped at a drugstore. I had a lot of scratches on my face and right arm, and at least two of them could probably have used a couple stitches. I knew they'd scar if I didn't keep the wounds pulled together, but I figured they were small enough to close with butterfly bandages. Yet another gem gleaned from years of boxing.

Chapter 4
DOWNHILL

I climbed out of the shower and toweled off. What a day. First Treadwell, then the wreck. I hoped there was no truth to the adage that bad luck comes in threes.

Cleaned up, I could finally do a good inspection. I had four or five small scratches on my face, plus a good gash on the forehead. My nose was puffy and red, my bottom lip was busted, and my right eye was beginning to hint at turning black. I flexed my right arm and leaned into the mirror to get a closer look at the myriad cuts on it.

I could see a tiny shard of glass in one of the gashes. I picked it out.

Standing up straight, I inspected the rest of my bruised torso. I'd always felt I was fairly well built, but I spent more time in the ring or with a punching bag than I did with the free weights, so my muscles were more long than bulky. As I looked in the mirror, I considered lifting heavier weights. Bet that would bulk me up.

"Hey man," Greg called from the living room. "Gil and Al are over at Famous Pub. I told 'em we'd come by before the Treadwell thing on the quad."

I came into the living room with just a towel wrapped around my waist. Greg was sitting cross-legged in front of my TV, lost in a video game.

"Check this out," I said.

Startled, Greg jumped up. "What the hell!"

I cracked up. "Check this out," I repeated, motioning at the line going from my left shoulder down to the right side of my stomach.

"Man, that's going to be ugly," Greg shook his head.

I had a perfect seatbelt strap mark running across and down my torso. The inside of the mark was bright pink, outlined sharply with a slowly forming bluish-purple bruise. It was uncomfortable, but it looked far worse than it felt.

"Go get your clothes on already," Greg said, turning back to the TV and un-pausing the game. "We've got things to see and people to do."

I headed back to the bedroom to grab some clothes. Glancing at the clock, I saw we had a couple hours before we were supposed to be back at the quad.

"Have you beaten this mission where you're supposed to kill the Korean drug lord?" Greg yelled from the other room.

"Yeah. It's a bitch isn't it?" I yelled back, tugging a polo shirt over my head.

"Friggin' impossible."

"Let me just check my email real quick," I said as I came back into the living room. "Then we can split."

"Whatever." He didn't look up.

What the hell? My laptop wasn't on the kitchen counter. The charger was there, but no computer. I went back to the bedroom, it wasn't on the dresser either. That was the only other place it would be.

Shit. Did I leave it in the car? It definitely wasn't in the stuff I took out of the car before Greg got there. But I went and rifled through the bag of stuff anyway. Nope, not there.

"Crap!" I howled. "No way. No freakin' way!"

"What, dude, what?"

"I think left my laptop in the car," I groaned. Then I thought for a moment. "No. You know, I don't think I did. I'm almost certain I left it here today, because I knew I wouldn't need it. I had everything I needed on a disk. Look—" I pointed toward the charger. "I always bring the charger with it."

"Oh man, that does suck," Greg commiserated. "Listen, I'll take you by the junkyard tomorrow and we'll see if we can find it there. You should get some pictures of the car for Facebook anyway."

"No, wait… It's not in the car. I'm sure of it." I had searched the car thoroughly, and I'd taken everything, even a ratty old pair of track shoes I should have thrown away months ago. There was no way I would have missed my laptop.

"Well, then you'll find it later. Let's go."

"Listen, it's missing. I've got to find it."

"Dude, in case you missed it, school is out. You're done with the semester. Better yet, you're done *for good*. You are now an Emory grad. Go buy three laptops as soon as you get a real job."

"I'm serious, Greg. What the hell happened to it? It's not here. It wasn't in the car…"

"Are you sure it wasn't in the car? Look at you—you're a mess, man," he said, shaking his head at me. "Maybe it flew out the window. That guy hit the hell out of you."

"Maybe." He was making sense. More sense than my computer just vanishing, anyway. I grinned at the craziness of the wreck. "I always keep my book bag in the front seat, and I found the freaking thing all the way behind the back seat!"

"See, there you go. Who the hell really knows where that thing could be? Let's just go, get some drinks, make up a few limericks, and sing songs about the great Tom Treadwell." He threw his arm around my shoulder. "Everything will be clearer to you in the morning."

He was right: no point in bothering with it right now. My neck had been feeling a little funny, and now it was beginning to feel somewhat prickly. In fact, I was beginning to feel little aches and pains all over.

I grabbed some painkillers from the kitchen—left over from when I busted a couple ribs last year—as we headed out the door.

Famous Pub is in the Druid Hills area and fairly close to campus, so it just naturally became kind of an Emory hangout. The front half was a huge bar and several booths; the back half had another bar plus about fifteen pool tables, a few arcade games, and a half dozen more booths. And everywhere you looked there were huge flat screens playing the big games of the day.

In the evenings it was packed, but it was four in the afternoon on a Monday and the place was dead.

Gil and Al were sitting at a booth near the front bar with a half-empty pitcher. There were two clean mugs waiting for us.

Gil looked shocked. "What the hell happened to *you?*"

I slid in and grinned. "You should see the other guy."

"What the fuck ever," Greg said, making a fist and pretending to examine his knuckles as he slid in. "I *am* the other guy."

It wasn't long before Greg launched into the story. Everything's always bigger and better when Greg tells it.

"So I get this call and Dale's like…"

Greg mocked me in the tone of a whining child: "'Can you *please* come pick me up? I've been in a little fender bender.'" His voice resumed a normal tone. "So I'm like, man whatever. Dale's my boy, I got his back. 'Sure I'll come pick you up.'"

He leaned toward Gil. "Anyway, I'm figuring no big deal. Just a fender bender, right? Well, I show up and there's like five cop cars and three ambulances. I'm like, what the hell? Then I see this car on a tow truck. Dude, the whole side is crushed in and the engine is gone! Friggin' gone, dude! I'm like holy shit, Dale just killed somebody. Nobody could survive that."

He looked around the table earnestly. "Nobody! So I get out of my car and walk toward a cop talking to the tow truck driver. Suddenly I realize: holy shit, that's *Dale's* car! Oh my God, he's dead."

Everybody was into the story, even me. I wanted to know if I was going to live.

Greg shook his head. His voice lost its excitement and turned apathetic. "Then I see Dale, just sitting by himself next to some pile of shit he took out of the car, like, 'Fodey doe.' Not a scratch on him."

He went on to talk about all the traffic helicopters hovering overhead and how I had snarled traffic on Ponce.

A few minutes later Dave and Sam showed up. Naturally Greg had to tell the story again—only this time it was even more exciting.

These guys were all brothers from the same house. They had asked me to pledge long ago, but fraternities just weren't my thing. Plus, I never had time or money as it was. I could go to their parties whenever I wanted anyway, so why bother with all the other bullshit? I just wasn't much for team play, I guess. Hence boxing, instead of, say, football or baseball.

The booths around us began to fill up with classmates. Somehow word had passed that Famous was the unofficial pre-meeting place for Treadwell's unofficial memorial.

Soon the conversation turned to Treadwell, my accident was quickly forgotten, and the mood turned somber.

I still couldn't believe Mr. Treadwell was dead. When I'd seen him last week, he'd been perfectly fine. I guess you just never know.

At the same time, I couldn't help but feel happy to be done with school forever. And that made me feel guilty. Was it wrong to feel happy for myself? And I wasn't just a little happy. To be honest, I felt like getting totally hammered, ripping all my clothes off, and running through the streets shouting, "Hooray!"

A horrible tragedy, starkly contrasted by consequent good fortune. What a dichotomy. Heartbroken and jubilant in the same instant.

And who *were* all these people? There must have been ninety somber people in the bar by the time Jessica herded us all out the door.

When we arrived on campus, our numbers were noticed, but not by much. There were over a thousand students and faculty members packed into the quad. There were even a half dozen or so reporters.

Wow. I guessed that made sense, though. Treadwell *had* been something of a celebrity.

Somebody had put a bunch of folding chairs in the middle of the quad, and for some reason the first five rows remained empty. A few moments later I found out why.

"May I have your attention please," asked the business school chancellor, Dr. Bernstein, as he took the podium. "At this time I would like to invite all of the students from Mr. Treadwell's New Venture Management classes to come forward and take the seats at the front."

Oh.

Man, what was going on? I had thought this was just going to be a super-informal gathering of classmates. Somehow it had turned into a full-on production. I wasn't so sure about all this.

I hung back in the crowd as my classmates moved to the front.

After giving all Treadwell's students a chance to settle

49

into their seats, the chancellor resumed. "Before we begin this evening, I have the unfortunate duty of announcing yet another tragedy." He paused, and I think the entire courtyard sucked in a collective breath. "Sadly, another of our esteemed alumni, a long-time friend and Emory benefactor, passed away early this morning. Dr. Miles Prestone suffered a major heart attack and is no longer with us. He will be dearly missed. May God rest his soul."

I knew that guy—he'd been one of the guys on Treadwell's panel of VC cronies. Wow, that sucked. And it was more than a little unsettling. Two guys I'd seen alive, just last week, both now dead and gone.

The chancellor asked that we all join him in singing a spiritual before he opened the floor for people to share.

I slipped away from the crowd. I don't deal well with death, and I really wanted a cigarette. Nobody was going to miss me.

I lit my smoke as I rounded the corner of the library. I had gone only a few feet when I saw Jessica sitting on a stone bench. I briefly considered beating a hasty retreat, but she had already spotted me.

She was leaning forward, sitting with her elbows on her knees, her hands tucked under her chin. As soon as my eyes met her tearful gaze, she buried her face in her hands. Crud.

Jessica and I weren't each other's biggest fans. She was cute—long brown hair, big brown eyes, and petite figure—but she was way too uptight for my taste. And it was quite clear from the way she treated me that she dismissed me as an inconsequential party boy.

Not knowing what else to do, I sat down next her on the bench and awkwardly put my arm around her. I was surprised when she responded immediately by leaning her head into my shoulder. My awkward attempt to console her became a natural, warm embrace.

Now I felt a twinge of regret for having laughed when others poked fun at her nerdy, type-A personality traits. She wasn't so bad.

She wasn't sobbing or anything, but I could feel her back tremble as she cried quietly. Man, she was really shaken up over this. I guess everybody reacts differently to death.

The singing stopped and I could hear a distant speaker, but couldn't make out what was being said. I extinguished my cigarette and made a failed effort to flick the butt into the waiting receptacle. The crowd broke into subdued laughter.

We sat listening to the distant sounds for a while without speaking. I realized that I, too, benefited from the shared solace.

After we had been sitting there for several minutes, she began to stir. She placed her hand on my chest and tilted her face up to look at me. Our noses were but inches apart. Her eyes filled with tears again and her lower lip began to tremble. With hushed, stumbling words she began to speak.

"I... I... I wished he would die! I wished they would all die." She blurted out her confession, then locked her eyes on mine, awaiting my condemnation. Suddenly I was in that hallway again, and Jessica was rushing out of the conference room after giving her New Venture pitch, tears running down her cheeks, nose in the air, hurrying down the hall.

"Oh my God," I said, chuckling. I tightened my arm around her and, with my left hand, gently pushed her face back toward my shoulder. "Listen to me. If you could really make stuff come true just by wishing it, I would have been a multimillionaire with a thousand concubines by the time I was twelve!"

She laughed despite herself.

"And look," I continued. "You're not alone in feeling that way. Treadwell and his little gang pissed everybody off. They told Greg that his idea was stupid. Can you believe that? Not 'gee, we don't think your proposal is feasible.' Not 'thank you for your time but we aren't interested.' No, they didn't waste any effort on nicety. They just said, 'dude, your idea is stupid.'"

"You're lying." She had pushed back and her eyes were now searching mine. She smiled quizzically. "They really said that?"

"I swear." I smiled sincerely. "One of those guys stood up right in the middle of my speech, threw my papers in the trash, and walked out! Believe me, a lot of people spent the week cursing those guys."

I saw no benefit in telling her how well my pitch ended up.

"Oh my goodness." She laughed. "So I wasn't alone. I was so embarrassed that everybody saw me crying."

"No, you definitely weren't alone. I heard that two other people came out crying. And the same thing happened in the MBA class." I shrugged. "Listen, those guys pissed everybody off. That's a lot of bad mojo. Maybe everybody wished they were dead at the exact same time and that's what got them."

The tears were gone and she was smiling in earnest. Then the smile faded away and she laid her head back on my shoulder. I suddenly became very conscious of the fact that I was sharing an intimate moment with Kermit. Go figure.

"He really was a very nice man," she said. I agreed in silence.

I was thinking about how Treadwell's class was one of those rare lecture classes in which I'd actually maintained perfect attendance. Not so much because I enjoyed the subject—although I did, immensely—but more because Mr. Treadwell was such an exciting and interesting person. I realized that I was very lucky to have known him, even if it was only for a brief moment.

"I heard you totaled your car earlier."

"Yeah." I suddenly felt very, very tired.

"Do you need a ride home?"

"You know, this is really weird… you being nice to me."
Maybe I shouldn't have said that.

She sat up straight and lightly punched my shoulder. I
tried not to show that she had landed on a particularly nasty
bruise. "Why does everybody think I'm such a bitch?"

"One issue at a time." She hit my bruise again.

My plan had been to go back over to frat row, do a bit
of drinking, and crash at Greg's place. But at this point, all I
wanted to do was crawl into bed.

"Yeah, I would really appreciate a ride."

"I'm ready whenever you are."

Dusk had fallen, and as we made our way behind the crowd
toward the parking lot, I could see that most everybody was
holding a lit candle. At that moment, the courtyard looked
like a small galaxy of stars, all dancing in the fading light.

Chapter 5
SPIRALING

J essica's Audi needed gas, so we stopped in at the same gas station where I had bought cigarettes earlier. She beat me to the pump with her card.

"I'm gonna grab a Coke, do you want anything?" I asked.

"I'll take a Diet Coke."

As I walked into the store, it felt to me like weeks had passed since I'd bought those cigarettes. But the same Middle Eastern guy that had been working this morning was still at the counter, reading a magazine. Amazing—my life had been turned upside down in the time it took for this guy to wait out a single, boring, all-day shift. He looked up as I came in and smiled briefly when he recognized a return customer.

I walked to the back, toward the freezers, and had been in the store for only a few moments when I heard the shout.

"Give me your fucking money!"

I was reaching for a Diet Coke.

"Please, sir! I give you no troubles! Just take the monies, sir! Please, I don't want—"

BANG.

Oh, Jesus.

Screeching tires. Time literally stood still. I hoped those had been Jessica's tires tearing out of here. Glass crashing in the front.

"Get him," came the strangely calm command.

A split second later, CRACK CRACK CRACK. In quick succession, the shots sounded sharper this time, but slightly muffled—as if they came from outside. Did they chase somebody down in the parking lot?

I was crouched behind an end cap at the back of the store. Please, please don't come back here. Another patron was crouching three end caps over from me. He was white as a sheet.

I cast about for anything that could be used as a weapon. There was a shelf full of pork-n-beans right in front of me. I briefly debated which would hurt more, a can of beans or the can of soda in my hand. The beans won.

A shuffling of feet. A grunt. The cash register opening.

"Check the back," ordered the same eerily calm voice.

No. My heart was pounding and my ears were ringing. The air was electric; the store seemed particularly bright; the world around me was sharply in focus. I was even conscious of the buzz from the fluorescent lights above. With nowhere else to go, nowhere else to hide, I stayed put.

I never heard him coming, but I didn't have to. I could see the other patron's face transform into sheer terror.

He cried out as the barrel of a shotgun became visible, pointed right at his face. "Oh God, *no!*"

BOOM.

And like that, a quarter of the man's head was transformed into unrecognizable meat. Chunks of bone and hair stuck to the wall behind him. He toppled over backward, not fifteen feet from me.

Suddenly I realized that I had leaped up when the gun went off and was now charging the opening where the gun barrel had appeared. As the assailant rounded the corner, I was already coming at him full tilt. My arm was fully extended above my head and arcing downward.

The can of beans, clenched in my hand, cracked into a ski-mask-covered head, right where the ear should be. The man went down like a sack of potatoes.

"Fuck!" he yelled.

In the movies, the guy would be conveniently unconscious after something like that—and definitely not yelling. Maybe I just didn't hit him right. The man grabbed my knee and tugged as I gathered up his shotgun.

I didn't lose my balance. We locked eyes, him staring up from the floor, me looking down over the barrel.

From the front of the store: "What?"

The moment broke. *BOOM.*

The force of the recoil shocked me. The man on the floor went limp, blood gushing from a massive hole in his chest.

"T?"

I backed away in a daze. Bumping into the door of the cooler brought me out of it.

"T!" The man yelled for his partner again. I could hear stuff fall off the counter as he leaped over it. I figured he was headed to check on his partner, so I ran quietly for the front of the store. Briefly I considered making a dash for the exit. No, too risky.

Instead, I moved quickly toward the aisle that the first thug had come down. I peered around the corner in time to see the second guy, with his back to me, edging toward the other end of the aisle, toward my old hiding spot. I strode forward, shotgun pointed square at his back.

He popped back suddenly, having seen his partner on the ground. And then he saw me.

"Shit."

I had him dead to rights.

But when I pulled the trigger, it was just slack. No click, no nothing. If I had simply pumped the shotgun, the spent shell would have ejected, another would have chambered, and I would still have him. But I panicked. Thinking I was out of ammo, I swung the shotgun at him full force, like a club.

He was down for the count. And from the sound of the wet crack when the butt hit his head, I figured he was dead. But I wasn't taking any chances.

I leaned over and pulled the large pistol out of his hand and ran out the front door. I went right past a dark sedan, reverse parked in the handicapped spot closest to the door with the engine running. I felt a brief shock of panic as I realized it was the getaway car, and that there might be another guy in it. But it was empty.

For the second time that day, I could hear distant approaching sirens. I arrived at Jessica's car to find the driver's side door open, but no Jessica. The car's warning bell was dinging to remind her that the keys were in the ignition.

I wanted to get the hell out of there. What if those guys were only stunned? I had no interest in waiting for the arrival of those sirens; I just wanted to run. But I couldn't leave without Jessica. Where the hell was she?

I had no choice but to wait. She was probably ten blocks away, running fast and hard to escape the gunshots she'd heard. I moved to the rear of her car and crouched down. From this vantage point I could watch the front of the store. If anyone came out, I could make a quick escape into the darkness behind me.

Somebody pulled into the station behind me. Not a cop car. It pulled into the spot right next to the getaway car. A new customer—totally oblivious to the situation.

As an elderly black lady climbed out of the car, I shouted at her, "Get back in your car! Get back in the car!"

She froze, one foot in the car, the other on the pavement, just staring at me. Instead of inspiring action, my words had just brought her to a confused standstill.

"Robbery!" I shouted. That did the trick. She tore out of there like a race car driver.

It was then that I noticed someone lying about thirty feet away, in the shadow between the filling station and the store. I studied it. It was a man, crumpled on the ground unnaturally, and not moving... not Jessica, thank God.

What in the hell were these guys thinking? People rob gas stations all the time, but they don't go on a rampage and kill everybody in the store. Killing a gas station clerk is one thing—maybe they thought he would press a silent alarm or something. But killing everybody in sight over a hundred lousy bucks is another matter entirely. That's just crazy.

I was trying to wrap my head around the senseless brutality when I felt a hand on my back. I swear to God I jumped right out of my skin.

It was Jessica, looking like she had just run a marathon.

"Stay low and get in the car." I motioned her toward the passenger side with the pistol in my hand. I had forgotten I was still holding it.

Before either of us could move, the second ski-mask-wearing bad guy, the one I'd clocked with the butt of the shotgun, came stumbling out. So I hadn't killed him. I doubted "T" was as lucky as his buddy. I tried to wipe that image from my mind.

I grabbed Jessica and pulled her down. My heart was pounding again as I mentally prepared for action.

The sirens were really loud now, and suddenly a police cruiser turned onto the street, not four blocks away.

The sound of squealing tires right in front of me jerked my attention back. The bad guy was getting the hell out of there.

I stood up and pointed, and the cruiser gave chase. Moments later two more cop cars went flying past, joining the pursuit. *Hello? What about us?*

One, then two more cruisers flew past without so much as a thought of turning in. I wanted to go check on the guy lying in the parking lot, but I was still afraid to expose myself. I was pretty damn sure that I had blown the other guy straight to hell, but I had thought his friend was done, too…until he came out and drove off.

A moment or two passed before an ambulance arrived. Then a police cruiser. Next thing I knew there were flashing lights all over the place.

Jessica explained to me that she had heard shouting in the store, had looked up, and saw a guy wearing a ski mask shoot the clerk. She wasn't sure what to do—she just wanted to get away and get away fast. In her panic, she didn't want to waste time climbing into the car, turning it on, getting it into gear—what if the engine didn't turn, like in the movies? —so she just ran.

As she ran, she heard gunshots that she was pretty sure were outside the store. Believing she was being shot at, she dove behind a dumpster. She had been hiding there the entire time, not two hundred yards away. Then after things had been quiet for a while, she peeked out, and saw me hiding behind her car.

Shortly after officials arrived on the scene, Jessica and I were put into two separate squad cars and taken to the Atlanta Police Department on North Avenue. I spent the next several hours in an interrogation room. Three different detectives talked to me. The second two pretty much asked me the exact same questions the first one had already covered.

No, I don't know him. He's just always there when I shop.
[picture of a dead clerk]
No, I've never seen him before.
[picture of a dead robber—the one I shot—his mask peeled back]
No, I don't know him.
[driver's license of the guy whose head got blown off in front of me]

59

No, I don't know him.

[another driver's license; guy in the parking lot?]

Why were you in the gas station? Where were you coming from? Where were you going? Ad infinitum.

I was unbelievably tired and I was quickly becoming sick of their questions. Every inch of my body was sore. Even the coffee they kept pumping into me wasn't helping. In fact, it was starting to become disruptive, because it was going right through me.

In the beginning I was really nervous because the tone of questioning was very suspicious. My assumption that I had actually killed a man was correct. Was I in trouble?

But the second detective was much nicer than the first. He had reviewed the tapes from the store's security camera, and went out of his way to assure me that I had clearly acted in self-defense and that no charges would be filed. I wasn't in any trouble, but this was a triple homicide and they needed to dot all the i's and cross all the t's. Just be patient, this will all be over soon.

I was in the middle of explaining to the third detective why Jessica was giving me a ride home when someone tapped on the window. The door opened and the detective was motioned out.

I sat there for a few minutes. After a while I lay my head on the table and tried to take a quick nap. But every time I closed my eyes, I could see the look of terror on the hiding customer's face. He had begged for his life. "Oh, God, *no!*"

BOOM.

In an instant, most of his head was gone. I wasn't sure how I felt about it yet. I wasn't sure if I felt anything. But there it was. And my mind insisted on replaying the gruesome scene over and over.

The door opened again and now a short, slight black man in his fifties, more sharply dressed than the others, came in. A fourth detective? Christ.

"Hello, Mr. Adams. My name is Agent Sparrows and I'm with the FBI," he said matter-of-factly, taking a seat. The FBI?

He got straight to the point. "Do you have any enemies?" What?

"What? Me? I don't think so." I was incredulous. "You can't possibly think this had anything to do with me?"

"Who is this?" Sparrows asked, sliding a picture across the table.

I recognized the face—thanks only to the three other detectives shoving that same face under my nose repeatedly over the course of the last few hours. Except in this photo, the guy was still alive. "It looks like that guy I killed."

"Yes, yes," he said, curtly. "That's the guy you killed. Look at his eyes and concentrate. Don't answer so quickly this time. Just look at him and focus on his eyes."

I did as requested. The man in the picture was maybe thirty-five, with blue eyes and short, clean-cut blond hair. No amount of concentration was going to help; I simply didn't know him.

"Listen, I just don't know the guy. I'm sorry."

He slid three more pictures across the table. "What about these men?"

I shuffled through them, taking a moment to inspect them one by one. A middle-aged guy, balding on top. An older man in a suit. An Asian guy with a big smile and dead eyes.

"Come on man," I pleaded. "Are they Emory professors or something? How the hell should I know them?"

Sparrows leaned forward. "This man"—he tapped the forehead of the guy I'd killed—"was being held in the Fulton Federal Penitentiary, awaiting an extradition hearing related to suspicion of murder-for-hire in Romania. He was released last week on a ten-million-dollar cash bond." He looked up at me, then back down. "This man," he continued, tapping the older man, "is his lawyer, and the one who posted the bond. The bond money came from this man." He tapped the bald guy. "And this one"—the Asian—"picked him up after he was released."

He sat back, hands behind his head, and just looked at me.

What the hell did all this shit have to do with me? Why the hell was he looking at me like I was in on some big secret?

"So my question to you is this: what the hell is an ex-Navy-SEAL-turned-mob-hit-man doing robbing a convenience store? He sits in jail, cooling his heels for over a month. Then suddenly someone drops a ten-million-dollar cash bond for him, and he pops up a few days later to knock over a gas station? Killing everybody in sight for, what, a hundred and fifty bucks worth of loot? Come on."

Yeah, that didn't make much sense.

"Look, sir, I understand your point." Unfortunately, I really did. "But believe me, you're talking to the wrong guy. If they were after someone, it wasn't me. It must have been the guy in the parking lot or the dude in the back of the store. It wasn't me. I was just in the wrong place at the wrong time," I said.

That was the God's honest truth. There was zero possibility anybody would pay ten dollars, let alone ten million, to have *me* killed. I knew it, and moreover, I knew the FBI agent knew this as well.

Still he questioned me for another half hour. Then he spent a half hour after that asking me about Jessica. My assertion that I barely knew her seemed to be hard for him to swallow. But eventually he left well enough alone.

Finally he left, and I languished in the brightly lit room for another forty-five minutes. By the time the first detective came back to lead me out, it was almost three in the morning.

I followed the detective to the lobby, where Jessica

was sitting with a man that I assumed must be yet another detective.

Where had I seen him before?

Chapter 6
PARANOIA

As soon as I arrived in the lobby, a uniformed officer informed us that he'd be giving us a ride back to Jessica's car.

I had been surprised to see that Jessica was still at the police station. I had figured her parents would have already come and picked her up. But it turned out that Jessica's parents lived in Los Angeles—and besides they were in Europe at the moment.

I felt really bad for her. She might've been tightly wound in everyday life, but her heart wasn't made of stone. She was already genuinely torn up over Treadwell's death, and then this. She didn't say a word on the way back to her car. Her eyes were red-rimmed and she seemed exhausted.

When our cruiser pulled up to the gas station, another officer moved the police barricade to let us through. Two "Crime Scene Investigation" vans were in the parking lot, along with about a half dozen people. The whole area was lit bright as day, as large portable lights, like the kind you see on a construction site, had been stationed all around the scene.

Jessica and I got in her car and pulled out. It wasn't until we were sitting at a light a few blocks away that she finally decided to speak.

"You killed one of those guys tonight," Jessica said quietly, staring straight ahead. It was a statement, not a question. I didn't say anything.

Honestly, I still hadn't had much time to process that. When it happened, I'd been looking right into the guy's eyes. And now, I wasn't sure how I was supposed to feel. You always hear about people coming back from war, haunted by the eyes of the people they had killed. I wasn't yet sure if I'd be troubled about having killed that guy. But the other guy, the one who'd begged for his life... I didn't think I'd ever get past that.

It was strange, I thought, to feel so torn up about seeing someone killed, but to feel so matter-of-fact about having killed someone myself.

Neither of us said anything the rest of the way back to my place. Jessica had been there a couple times before for study group in a finance class, so there was no need to give directions. She pulled into a parking spot in front of my apartment and turned off the engine.

"I don't want to go home," she said. "Can I please stay on your couch?"

"Of course."

* * *

Noise in the kitchen startled me out of a deep sleep. I could smell food and coffee. Why was I on the couch?

Then the previous day came back to me in a flash, and I realized it was Jessica in the kitchen.

I didn't say anything or get up—I just lay there thinking. Man, it seemed like I'd lived an entire life in one day. But the weirdest thing was what stuck in my mind: the man Jessica had been sitting with in the lobby the previous night.

As I lay there and thought about it, I suddenly remembered

why that man seemed familiar, and where I'd seen him before. He was the guy who'd first come up to my car window right after I'd gotten hit by that dump truck. He asked if I was okay, and then he just walked away. Seemed like weird behavior for a cop.

Maybe he wasn't a cop.

"Hey," I said, sticking my head over the end of the couch to look into the kitchen. "Last night, right before we left the police station... you were sitting with some guy in the lobby. Who was he?"

"Good morning to you, too," Jessica said, leaning over the breakfast bar with a spatula in her hand. She disappeared again, busy with a skillet. "He was a policeman. I talked to him a little bit when I first got to the station, then again for a moment before you came out."

"Was he an Atlanta cop or FBI?"

"How should I know? He didn't say. He just asked if I was okay, if you were okay, whatever. Seemed more like he was making small talk. I thought he was a little strange."

"Why do you say that?"

"I got the feeling he was hitting on me. Seemed like a weird thing to do, considering."

She leaned back across the counter to take another look at me. "Jesus, you're a mess!"

"I bet it feels worse than it looks," I moaned, laying my head back on the couch.

My neck was absolutely killing me. Was this whiplash? I'd always thought whiplash was something lawyers had invented to give themselves a reason to live. But this *really* sucked. I could barely hold my head up. My whole body felt like a giant toothache, and my head was throbbing. And I felt disgustingly filthy to boot.

When we'd arrived at my apartment, I had been so tired that I'd simply showed Jessica to my room, grabbed a blanket,

66

stripped to my boxers, and crashed on the couch. No shower, no new clothes, nothing. I just turned off like a light.

I had at least washed up a bit when I'd arrived at the police station, using paper towels to wipe off what I assumed was blood spray off my face and hands as best I could. Now I was second guessing the thoroughness of that cleaning, and wondered if I was wearing any pieces of the guy I shot.

Oh God, I killed a man yesterday.

"Breakfast is served," Jessica said dramatically. My stomach turned. "How do you take your coffee?"

"Black," I answered, slowly pushing myself off the couch. What did I do with those painkillers? I slid into the pants I was wearing yesterday and rifled through the pockets. Bingo.

Jessica placed a cup of joe next to a plate of eggs and toast on the counter. I tossed a pill in my mouth and took a cautious sip of coffee to help wash it down. Jessica watched me with a shocked expression.

I knew what she was seeing: a huge seatbelt bruise across my torso, a big shiner of a black eye, a puffed-up red nose, and various other cuts and bruises. Not a pretty sight, I'm sure. I'd been banged up worse before, but at the moment I was hard pressed to think of when.

I took my coffee and headed for the sliding glass door. I lived on the second floor and had a little deck with an old charcoal grill, a few plastic chairs, and a small table.

As soon as I was outside, I lit a cigarette. It was a cool May morning, and I would have been chilly in the light breeze were it not for the direct sunshine. I had left the sliding door open for Jessica, and now she joined me, carrying a glass of water and two plates. Had she made the coffee just for me?

"Thank you," I said, feeling bad for not bringing my plate. "I guess I wasn't ready for breakfast. I really need a shower first."

"That's okay, it'll be here when you're ready for it."

As she turned to sit down, I realized she was wearing one of my old T-shirts like it was a small nightgown. I don't know if it was just that look of a girl in an oversized T-shirt or what... but she was definitely not looking like a frog.

She seemed content to just sit in silence and eat. The silence was perfect. I felt an unexpected comfort in her quiet company.

And, Lord forgive me, but how I *love* a good cup of joe and a cigarette in the morning. I don't think I realized how much I had missed smoking until this moment. When I finished the cigarette, my coffee was still half-full, so I lit another.

"What made you think about that guy?" Jessica asked curiously.

My thoughts went back to the strange cop. "Last night I recognized him, but couldn't figure out from where. This morning I remembered that he was at my accident yesterday," I answered.

"That's a weird coincidence. No wonder he was asking so many questions about you. Maybe he's an accident investigator," she mused.

"No, I don't think so," I said. The more I thought about it, the more it bothered me. "That's what's so strange about it. I'm pretty sure he was in the car right behind me when the dump truck hit me. It's not like he showed up with the other cops; he was already there. He was the first person to the car, asked if I was okay. I said yes and was going to ask him to help me out, but when I looked up he was gone. He just walked away and never came back."

"Okay, now that really *is* weird. You'd think he'd at least wait for other cops to arrive before leaving."

It really did seem strange. Maybe he had to respond to the scene of some crime or something and couldn't stay. But I was covered in blood, and there was no way for him to know how bad I was hurt. You'd think he would've at least tried to help a bit.

"This FBI guy, Agent Bluebird or something—"

"Sparrows," I interjected with a chuckle.

"That's the one," she said with a smile. "Anyway, he was asking if you had any enemies that I knew of. Like the robbery was an attempt to kill you or something."

"Yeah, I know." I smiled back at her. "He asked me that stuff, too. Pretty funny."

While we considered it, I finished off my second cigarette, and was hit with a wave of hunger. I decided to go ahead and eat.

"Actually it's not a bad plan, if you think about it," I said, my mouth full of scrambled eggs. "If those guys were trying to kill a specific person in the store, then the assassination would have just looked like a robbery gone bad."

We were both silent for a while.

"I got it," she proclaimed. "What if Tom's death, the death of that other Emory guy, and the robbery last night are all linked! What if somebody is killing people and trying to make it all seem accidental?"

I looked up to find her smiling playfully.

"Yeah, it's the Emory Serial Killer…" I said. "Film at eleven." We both laughed.

I heard my cell phone ringing in the other room. I groaned as I struggled to get up. Jessica saw me having trouble, popped up, and scooted inside to grab my phone. I caught a glimpse of pink panties as she turned to go.

For crying out loud, Dale. It's Kermit. Get a grip.

"Dale's phone," I heard her say as she returned to the deck. Then, like a receptionist at a place of business, she continued, "Yes he is, hold please." She placed her hand over the mouthpiece. "Sir, there's a Mr. Greg Bates on the line. Would you like to speak with him, or shall I tell him you're in a meeting?"

I cracked up.

"Ah, Master Bates," I said with deep thought. "Why yes, I think I will speak to him."

"I told you it wasn't him, some chick answered the phone," Greg was yelling to someone on the other end. Then to me, irritably: "Dude, I heard that Master Bates bit. You know I hate that shit." His tone turned more conspiratorial. "So who's the chick? I wondered why you bailed on me last night. Do I know her?"

I was silent for a moment as I considered whether or not to tell him. He continued, "You were chasing a little trim, eh? Little sookie sookie… little nookie nookie… wink wink, nod nod… knowwhatImean, knowwhatImean…"

"Shut up, dude," I growled, interrupting his Monty Python routine. "It was Jessica."

She was watching me intensely. I wondered what was going through her mind.

"Osgood!" He practically shouted. I was sure she could hear him. "Okay, okay. I can see that. She's kinda sexy in that nerdy, schoolmarm kinda way. I always heard that the quiet librarian types get freaky in the sack…"

"Come on, dude." Now I was really embarrassed. Jessica had heard every bit of that, despite my efforts to muffle him.

"Tell ol' Kermy I say hi. You're busy, so I'll let you go," he finished.

"Okay." I didn't feel much like talking anyway. "Real quick, why did you call?"

"Oh, nothing now. I knew it wasn't you. This dumb-ass Gil just told me he heard on the news that some guy named Dale Adams killed a guy in a grocery robbery."

I heard somebody yell a correction in the background.

"It was a gas station," I said quietly, agreeing with the

correction.

Long pause.

"That was you? For real?"

Another long pause, while I considered how to admit it was me but still get off the phone.

"Yes, it was me. I'm all right. Everything is fine. I'll give y'all a call later, cool?"

"Yeah, that's cool," he said, very subdued.

The moment I hung up the phone, it started ringing again. I checked the caller ID—on the cracked screen—and saw it was another friend I didn't feel like talking to. I switched the phone to silent.

I hadn't considered that my name might be in the news. Atlanta has its share of crime and has some pretty rough neighborhoods, but a triple homicide is a big story even in a jaded city like the A. And actually, since I had killed one of the robbers, it was four people dead in a single incident. This was bound to be a news event.

I retired to the shower and Jessica switched on the tube.

"They say the guy who got away shot four cops, and killed two of them," she reported as I returned in a fresh polo and jeans. "And they're calling you a hero."

"Really? That's the stupidest thing I ever heard. Pretty much everybody died and the bad guys got away."

She was looking at me funny as I combed my still-wet hair with my fingers. What... did I have a booger on my chin or something? Behind her, the TV had been muted, but there was a picture of a familiar face on the screen.

"What the hell? Where's the remote?" I asked, spotting it on the couch even as I spoke.

"Oh my God," exclaimed Jessica as she turned and recognized the face right away.

I clicked off the mute so we could hear the Fox 5 news

report.

"...was known locally as the owner of Lou's Blues Review in Buckhead." The screen flashed to a scene of a horribly mangled car that had come to a rest beneath a sign reading I-285, lit by red and blue flashing lights. After a moment the view changed to a reporter standing outside Lou's Blues Review.

"A source at the DeKalb police has told Fox 5 that a note was found in the vehicle. Mr. Evans was apparently distraught over a pending divorce, and it appears that this single-car accident may indeed have been a suicide. Reporting live from Buckhead, I'm Mark Gold."

"Thanks for that live report, Mark."

The anchor continued talking, but I wasn't listening. Jessica was looking at me with alarm. "What's going on?"

"Go get dressed," I said. Suddenly I wanted to get out of here. I didn't know where I wanted to go, just anywhere but here.

It felt like all of the pieces came together at once. First, Mr. Treadwell and his wife died in a carbon monoxide accident. Then Dr. Miles Prestone dies of a heart attack. I almost get killed in an accident where the other driver mysteriously disappears, and then I almost get killed *again* by a real-life hit man during a staged robbery. And now Keith Evans, another of Treadwell's investors, commits suicide?

It was all too much. I suddenly felt very, very paranoid.

While Jessica was in the bathroom changing back into her own clothes, I busied myself by removing books from my duffel bag to lighten the load.

"Where are we going?"

"I don't know. Let's just get out of here. I'll figure it out," I said. I wasn't so sure about that.

Out of habit I went to the kitchen to grab my laptop,

then remembered its strange disappearance. Suddenly my hair stood on end.

Holy shit.

Chapter 7
MANUEL'S TAVERN

O ur departure was well timed: a Channel 2 Eyewitness News van was pulling into the complex even as we pulled out.

Our first stop was Jessica's place, so she could shower and change. Her roommate kept saying "Oh my God" like a valley girl, so I decided to wait outside with a cigarette.

While I waited, I tried to make sense of all the carnage. What if my car accident was no accident? What if the gas station robbery was nothing but a way to kill me, while disguising the fact that it was a hit?

A "hit." Come on! Like anybody would really put a "hit" on me. That kind of stuff happens to gangsters in movies, not useless college kids in the real world.

But... what if? That FBI guy said somebody paid ten million dollars to spring that hit man out of jail. What if they did that just so he could kill... me?

This was crazy. But there were just too many coincidences, abrupt deaths, and strange occurrences. This was way beyond the point where I could just brush it all off as bad luck.

Okay, fine. Something was afoot. But what? And more important: why?

Then I started thinking about the fact that my computer

had been stolen. Why the hell would somebody want my computer? All it had was a bunch of homework, reports, presentations, a couple video games, emails, and a bookmark or two to Girls Gone Wild online.

My laptop seemed a little too boring to warrant stealing. Maybe they were looking for more information about *me*. Then I wondered what else they took from my apartment. I'd never bothered to look.

My head was throbbing again.

If somebody wanted me dead, they could have easily done it right then. Jessica lived off campus in an area between Little Five Points and the Highlands. And I was standing right out in the open in the parking lot behind her building at Highland and North Avenue.

Just as I was reaching the height of my paranoia, a car pulled into the parking lot twenty feet away and stopped abruptly. It began easing toward me and the tinted window behind the driver slid down. Oh God, nowhere to hide.

"Hi! We're looking for the Carter Center," announced a lady in the back seat. Her brows furrowed with confusion at my expression.

"Oh," I said with relief. "You're very close. I think there's an entrance a few blocks that way."

As I pointed them in the right direction, I noticed a guy walking a Chihuahua. I had seen him earlier; now he was back and looked over at me while I gave directions.

Okay, now I was definitely losing it. I was going completely insane. The only thing at all weird about the guy was that he was big—I mean pro-baller big—and walking a tiny little dog.

Relax, man. He was probably just some gay guy minding his own business. He sure was a big guy though. Man, I felt bad for the catcher on his team. I bet he could eat that dog with a single bite.

I suddenly realized I was starved. That tiny breakfast

wasn't cutting it. What had I eaten yesterday? I hadn't had dinner or lunch. The only thing I could remember eating the whole day was a bagel before class.

Hell, *I* could probably have eaten that guy's dog with a single bite.

Jessica made her way toward me carrying a bag. The trunk of her Audi opened as she approached. The big guy was gone.

"Hey, I'm starved," I said. "Let's walk over to Manuel's."

"We just ate!"

"Yeah, well..."

Manuel's Tavern was catty-corner to Jessica's building. A squat building, it'd been built mostly out of granite carved off Stone Mountain.

I loved Manuel's. It was one of Atlanta's best-kept secrets. As you stepped inside, the nicotine-stained walls and obligatory beer can collection above the bar could easily fool you into believing you were in a typical hole-in-the-wall canteen—albeit one with better-than-average food. But there was a lot of southern history in the place, for those who knew. I always liked to think the ghosts of Lewis Grizzard and Ludlow Porch were still cutting up in the corner booth.

"I'll have a Loaded Dogzilla and a sweet tea," I told the waitress. She was a cute little hippy chick with a nose ring.

"I just want a water, thanks."

The waitress left, and Jessica turned to me thoughtfully. "So, did you figure it out yet?"

Death. Carnage. Paranoia.

"No," I answered simply. Then, with more trepidation, I said, "Well, actually... You're probably going to think I'm going schizoid on you, but I'm beginning to think that the gas station really did have something to do with us. Well—me, anyway. I was nearly killed twice yesterday. Plus, somebody stole my laptop."

"Um yeah…" Jessica said hesitantly. "You gotta admit, that does sound kind of paranoid. What makes you think someone stole your computer?"

I'd forgotten she didn't know about that yet, so I filled her in on the details. When I finished, Jessica thought for a moment then said, "Okay, let's assume somebody's killing people from Treadwell's panel of investors. And now the same person is trying to kill you. *And* this person stole your computer. Seems pretty obvious what's going on."

She paused, waiting for me to jump in. I had been thinking the same thing, but it just seemed so far out there.

"It has to be your New Venture pitch," she said, giving voice to my thought. "What was your idea? It must have been pretty extreme if someone's willing to kill over it."

"I pitched them on a skateboard that doesn't need wheels," I said simply. Jessica stared at me blankly. Aside from Treadwell's panel, I hadn't told anyone about my discovery. Now I decided to tell Jessica the whole story—starting from the very moment that first can of Coke shot into the ceiling.

When I finished, she was staring at me like I was a Martian.

"Wow," she said at last. "My idea was to start a company that delivers giant blocks of ice to cool people's pools in the summer."

I burst out laughing. And instantly regretted it.

"Wow," I repeated, trying to recover with a show of enthusiasm. "I love it! I can't stand diving into a pool that's warm as piss. I bet that would take off like wildfire! In the South, especially."

"Thanks." She smiled sarcastically. "You don't have to be nice about it. Believe me, I know it's stupid."

"No, I'm serious! I think it's a great idea."

She could tell I was being genuine. She smiled sadly. "Listen, nobody kills people over swimming pool ideas."

She was right. Leading up to my presentation, I remember

thinking—actually, *knowing*—that I was on to something huge. I had read everything I could find about magnets, gravity, and electricity. I'd stumbled onto a bunch of hopelessly complicated information about some surfer searching for a unified Theory of Everything and a theoretical particle called a graviton that was supposed to tie everything together.

"Hello?" Jessica interrupted my thoughts. "Well, did they like your presentation? You told me they hated it. Were you just trying to cheer me up?"

"No, no. They did hate it," I said, remembering. "At first, anyway. I guess they thought it was some fraternity prank. That guy Michael Simons got all insulted and walked out of the room right in the beginning of my presentation. But then I broke out my skateboard, and that turned the tables. At the end of the talk, Treadwell said they wanted to talk to me after Monday's class… and, of course, he turned up dead on Monday."

She studied me for a long time, then smiled. "You're not quite as dumb as you look."

"And you think you're actually funny." I grinned at her. Okay, she's kind of cool. "Anyway, this is actually a big deal. I could use it to create all kinds of very cool products, like batteries that last forever, ships that can get into orbit without jet fuel, cars that don't need engines, cars that fly…"

"Oh, come on," she laughed. "Get serious. Flying cars, space ships, little green men?"

"I *am* serious," I snapped. "And I put it all in my paper, under Future Product Lines."

Jessica's face struggled to find an expression that wouldn't seem rude. But her eyes betrayed the truth. "Come on. A floating skateboard, maybe. But…"

"Look, I've been playing with this thing for a few weeks now. One of the first things I did was to test how much weight it could support. I put some aluminum on the bottom of a two-foot square of plywood, and set it up to hover. While it was in the air, I put a huge stack of bricks on it. It didn't even sink down a millimeter. Then I climbed on top the bricks, too. That's where the idea for a skateboard came from. But no matter what I did, I couldn't find a limit." I paused. "Listen, this is some kind of completely new property of physics."

Her eyes were still skeptical.

"Fine, don't believe me. But I put a link to my YouTube account in their copy of my business plan," I said. "And judging by the body count, somebody must've looked at it."

"What's your YouTube username?"

I gave it to her. She tapped it into her phone.

"There, that one," I said, pointing to the thumbnail on her screen.

She selected the video and set the phone down.

Just then the food arrived, and I dug in. I couldn't believe how hungry I was. The Dogzilla is a giant hot dog, piled high with chili, cheese, kraut, onion, and relish, but right now it looked just right for a snack. As I added some Tabasco, I wondered which was bigger, that dude's Chihuahua or my Dogzilla.

I ate while Jessica watched the video. I didn't need to watch; I knew exactly what she was seeing. On her phone, I was holding up a panel of quarter-inch plywood cut into a two-foot square. The video showed me slowly spinning it around in front of the camera for inspection. Sheets of aluminum foil had been hot glued to one side of the board, covering it completely.

Setting the board in the gravel, aluminum side down, I had picked up the camera and panned it along the path of an attached wire that connected the board to a small black box. It was the same box I had attached to the skateboard. Then the camera jiggled a bit as I'd set it down on the ground.

I grinned at Jessica through a mouthful of dog,

79

anticipating what was about to happen.

The camera just sat there for a few moments—the black box in the foreground, and the board two feet directly beyond. I probably should have edited this part out, but I wanted it to be clear that there were no camera tricks. Jessica's phone was turned up loud enough that I could hear it: the sound of an engine starting in the background, then the sound of gravel crunching as the front passenger tire of my Celica rolled into view and onto the board, filling the screen.

The engine cut off and a car door could be heard closing in the background. After another brief pause, my hand became visible, hovering just above the red button.

I laughed as Jessica gasped, seeing the front tire of my car being lifted effortlessly into the air. The video showed the levitation for another ten seconds, then faded to black.

"Jesus," she said under her breath.

"Yeah, I know," I said, stuffing another bite in my mouth. "Pretty cool, huh?"

Jessica stared at the blank screen in silence.

"Hey," I said with sudden realization, trying to swallow my bite so I could talk. "Nobody knows *how* I'm doing it. It's not even possible anybody could! I never wrote it down, let alone put it in my computer. I have the only working prototype in the bag I brought." I paused, thinking about the implications. "So if they're trying to kill me and they don't even know how it works... maybe they don't care. Maybe they don't want the technology. Maybe they just want to stop it."

Jessica looked up at me, but remained quiet for a moment. Finally she asked, "But why?"

"I don't know," I answered, finishing my dog. "Seems like a good thing to me. You could easily make a floating car out of it just by sticking one board under each tire, then adding another board at one end, a little lower than the others and at an angle. If you gave it juice, it would shove up and at an

80

angle, pushing the floating car forward. I haven't tried it yet because I don't know how I'd stop it. That's actually a huge flaw in the skateboard design: there's no way to stop it short of jumping off." I laughed. "But I think all you'd need is a board on the front of the car to counter it."

Jessica had the same expression those VC guys had when the skateboard had first floated on the table.

"Imagine a world with no gasoline. No need for gasoline if you don't need an engine. How about power plants that don't need coal or nuclear material? Better yet, what if we didn't need power plants because every house ran on its own everlasting battery?"

Jessica's eyes were wide.

"Even better than that," I continued. "What if houses didn't need wires and plugs, because every device had its own permanent, cheap, environmentally safe supply of power?"

Jessica shook her head violently. "This isn't real! This is a *floating skateboard*. You did not just solve the world's energy crisis. All this is, is a really neat toy."

Okay, maybe I was getting carried away with the whole thing. It actually felt kind of good to hear the voice of reason.

"Nobody is trying to kill us," she continued quietly. "This is just a really nasty run of luck, with a lot of really terrible tragedies. But it's nothing more than coincidence."

I felt a weight lifting off my shoulders. She was right. Reality. This was all too farfetched.

"What do we really know?" Jessica asked. She didn't wait for an answer. "Our professor and his wife died in a very sad carbon monoxide accident. One of the guys on the panel had a heart attack. Another guy committed suicide. Your computer is missing. And you had two scary experiences in one day."

We sat there looking at each other. Suddenly I felt a lot better.

"Well, when you put it like that." I gave a self-conscious chuckle. "Okay, I'm being silly. Yesterday was just a really long day, and I'm not thinking right."

I smiled feebly and pushed my french fries around. As goofy as I felt for giving voice to my delusions, I did feel a lot better. Her summary of the facts was much better than my paranoid slip-'n'-slide.

Just like that, order had been restored, and life made sense again. Jessica must have been thinking I was completely off my rocker to even dream that some idea I came up with could change the world.

"We're both not thinking right," she said gently. Then she smiled sheepishly. "You want to hear something really silly? You know that bag I brought to the car? A few days' worth of clothes... like we were going to make a break for the border or something."

Now we both had a good laugh. What strange tricks your mind will play during stressful times.

"I've got one for you," I announced, still chuckling. "Right before you came down, I almost ran away from some poor lady who just needed directions. I swear I thought she was there to kill me."

I finished my plate in silence. Wow. I'd never finished off a whole Dogzilla before. I must have been even hungrier than I realized.

I reached into my pocket for my cell phone. The cracked screen read: *14 MISSED CALLS.*

I wondered if there were reporters camped outside my apartment. *Man, this sucks.* I had just finished school, and I should have been enjoying myself. Real life was about to start. In a few weeks fun time would be over, and I'd be a faceless cog in some corporate machine.

Sublime's *Doin' Time* was playing over the speakers.

It wasn't fair to have this crap dumped on my life at this

moment. I just wanted to celebrate without a care. I wondered what Greg and them were up to.

But before I could dial Greg's number, the Carter Center lady sat down in the booth right across from us—with the Chihuahua giant.

The blood drained from my face. Sublime muted into the background as the world closed in around me. Jessica's voice sounded like a distant echo: "What?"

I struggled to keep my cool. We had just come to the conclusion that all the crazy events were just a long string of coincidence and bad luck, right?

This is just a coincidence, too. The lady I'd given directions to earlier, and some guy who had been loitering around with a dog—two people with seemingly no connection to one another—were now sitting at a booth directly across from us. Together.

Just a coincidence. *Keep it together, man. Don't be paranoid. Logic. There* is *a logical explanation here.* Why were they staring at me?

"How was the Carter Center?" I managed to get out.

Our waitress brought menus over for the new arrivals, but the big guy waved her off.

"It was fine, Dale, just fine," answered the lady. Any color left in my face was now gone.

Jessica turned to face the couple. "Friends of yours? Hi, I'm Jessica."

Both faces remained expressionless. Neither so much as acknowledged Jessica.

"No, I don't know them," I answered quietly, still looking the strange lady in the eyes. "I gave her some directions earlier."

I could tell Jessica's mind was in overdrive, attempting to weave logic into this crazy situation. How did this woman know my name?

"Are... are you with the FBI?" Jessica asked.

"No, ma'am," answered the lady, finger to her ear. Listening to something?

"I got it," said the big guy, drawing a pistol from his shoulder holster. He left the table and made his way to the front of the restaurant quickly.

Our waitress was making her way toward us, but must have noticed something amiss, as she quickly turned and beat a hasty retreat. I glanced back at the Carter Center woman and saw what had spooked the waitress: our lunch guest was now casually holding a pistol across her lap. I heard plates crashing to the floor as the waitress rounded the corner.

"Are you going to kill us?" came Jessica's apprehensive words.

The muffled sound of a gun blast cut off any answer. It came from outside. Then another shot. Suddenly a full barrage of gunfire. Someone in another room screamed, and others began shrieking in terror. It sounded as though a Fourth of July celebration was taking place right outside the bar.

We had to get out of there.

No sooner had I jumped up than I found myself lying flat on my face on the floor. What the hell was that? The lady had moved so fast that all I saw was a blur, then floor. And now she was on top of me, her knee jammed into my back, pistol pressed to the back of my head. *Fuck. I should have switched to MMA years ago.*

"Don't even think about it," she told Jessica. How could this lady be so calm? "Look, we're safe here for the moment. In a minute I'll get you guys out of here."

More gunfire, now automatic. Jesus, machine guns? Suddenly a huge thud, and the whole building shook. Then another thud, followed by the sounds of high-power electrical lines grounding out. A transformer exploded and all the lights went out in the bar.

"Please get off of me," I groaned.

My painkiller was wearing off, my neck was in agony, and this lady's knee was only exacerbating the situation. I was surprised when she actually complied.

There was a lull in the gunfire, then a single shot, followed by two more. Then silence. I struggled to my feet with Jessica's help. The lady had backed away and was now standing with her back to the bar, where she could watch both me and the front of the building.

She had dropped me with no more effort than if she were taking down a toddler. And she was holding a pistol. I saw no point in launching an attack or making a break for it, so I just stood right where I was.

Jessica clung to me. And not that I would wish this unending nightmare on anyone, but I was very glad not to be alone in this mess.

"Roger. Out the back in thirty," the stranger told the air. Then turning to us: "Move."

She herded us toward the back of the club. "Stop."

We were in front of a glass door at the back, with a little winding staircase to our left. Outside I could see a half dozen cars in the parking lot, but no people.

Suddenly the big guy was there, his shirt covered in blood. Another guy with an assault rifle rounded the corner and joined him.

"Go." The lady pushed us out.

We ran behind the big guy, cutting through the back parking lot and toward Jessica's apartment. Someone's car had taken out a telephone pole on North Avenue. Smoke was still pouring out of the crumpled engine compartment. The driver's door was slightly ajar and an arm was dangling out. Across the street, another car had crashed into Manuel's Tavern. This car was completely riddled with bullets.

Christ. It looked like a war zone out here.

Off to the right, a man was kneeling behind a bus stop bench with an assault rifle. A similarly armed man was kneeling about thirty yards away, covering the other direction. If not for the assault weapons, I would have taken these guys for run-of-the-mill businessmen, with plain gray suits and power ties.

Since our party never missed a step, I guessed the kneelers were friendly.

"Nine o'clock," said the big guy.

All three of the strangers drew up, but I had zero intention of stopping. I grabbed Jessica's hand. There was no need for me to encourage her though—she never broke stride either. Sirens everywhere.

"Your keys!" I shouted. She pressed them into my hand as we entered the parking lot behind her building.

"Wait!"

The lady was right on our heels, pointing a pistol at us. We stopped.

"Listen, if you want to live, you'll come with me."

She didn't wait for a response. She turned to her right and walked straight over to a car that I presumed was hers. It was the one she'd been in when she'd asked for directions. More gunfire out on the street. Were they shooting at cops?

As we approached, she opened the driver's door and turned to climb in. I seized the opportunity and landed what must have been the hardest punch I've ever thrown right on the side of her face. The top half of her body flung over so hard that her head bounced off the car with a sickening *thwack*.

Okay, yes. I hit a woman.

It was the first time in my life I had ever done something like that. And, man, did I hit her hard. During my years of boxing, twice I had managed to knock a guy out in the ring. I don't think I hit either of them half as hard as I'd just hit her.

"Come on!" I turned to find Jessica halfway to her car. Apparently she had no qualms about what I'd just done.

I dashed after her and jumped into the driver's seat, cranked the car, and tore off across the parking lot. I turned left onto North without even looking. The tail end of the Audi slung around as I whipped a left onto Moreland. Right onto Ponce, then ducked onto a smaller street that cut through the neighborhoods just after Paideia.

I risked a glance in the rearview mirror. There was no sign of anyone following.

I didn't slow down.

Chapter 8
STONE MOUNTAIN

As soon as I was off the main roads, I forced myself to drive at a less conspicuous speed. I knew the back roads through this primarily residential area very well. Because the traffic was so light and because I was making lots of turns, I was now able to be certain that no one was behind us. We went through Avondale and popped out onto I-285 at Indian Creek. A quick dogleg over and we were on 78 West, headed away from town.

Only ten minutes had elapsed, but we were already outside of the city and putting even more distance behind us at a good clip.

We had been extremely tense, riding along in silence, each lost in thought. Suddenly Jessica began laughing. And I mean, *really* laughing. Uncontrollably.

"Um, just out of curiosity," I began tentatively, "what exactly is so funny?"

"They're trying to kill us!"

I considered that for a moment. Nope, not funny.

I was reminded of my mother's funeral. She was Baptist. Actually, let me qualify that. She was *Southern* Baptist and very active with the church. Legally I was an adult when she passed, but I was still very young, so some of her church friends helped me to make arrangements.

The funeral ceremony itself was, naturally, held at the church. Mom, soft spoken as she was, was well loved, and pretty much the whole congregation turned out. There was a little sermon, followed by lots of joyful singing and praising. I was asked to say a few words, and then they opened the floor so that others could speak.

The first person to talk was my mom's best friend, Judith. Judith and Mom had been as close as sisters ever since I was a little boy. Judith spoke with a lisp, but I had known her for so long that I barely even noticed it.

My mom's name was Leslie. This posed quite an obstacle for someone with a speech impediment, which was made even worse by emotions and the fact that Judith was nervous to be standing before a large crowd to express her love. As she struggled with my mom's name for the fifth time, I suddenly found it amusing.

Amusing quickly transformed into flat-out funny. And then funny was replaced with hilarious. I burst out laughing right in the middle of a funeral for my own mother. I knew it was unbelievably inappropriate, but I couldn't help it. I hung my head and covered my face, hoping people would just think I had a weird way of crying.

Judith resumed speaking. Her words were warm, caring, and ever so sweet. I told myself to focus on her words, to listen to the nice things she was saying about my mother. My mother was dead. There was nothing funny about this.

Then Judith said "Leslie" again. That was it. She'd pushed me over the brink. I simply could not stop laughing! I rushed out of the church, my face covered in shame.

As I watched Jessica dry her eyes, I realized I was seeing a reflection of myself at Mom's funeral. Way too much pent-up emotion, with nowhere else to go, will escape any way it can.

"I bet enrollment would drop if Emory published its new

grading scale." Her laughter had stopped just long enough for her to speak. "4.0, 3.0, and *death!*"

She was rolling with laughter again. It still wasn't funny, but I couldn't help myself. I found myself laughing with abandon as well.

A sign said Memorial Drive. I decided to exit.

"Look," I said as we rolled into Old Stone Mountain. "They want *me*, not you."

She thought about this as I parked the car in a lot next to the railroad. I felt pretty comfortable that no one would think to look for us here.

"I think we should split up," I said. "You can be at the airport in half an hour. Just go home to California for a few weeks, until graduation."

She was quiet.

"What will *you* do?"

"I don't know," I answered wearily. "I'll figure something out."

Again she was quiet.

"They're going to kill you."

I didn't respond. She was right, and I knew it. It's very difficult to acknowledge that your life expectancy could be measured in hours—but that's all I had left; I was certain of it.

I had been extremely lucky over the last two days. A dog wandering into the road—a one-in-a-million fluke—had prevented a dump truck from hitting my car the way it should have. Then hours later, I somehow managed to get the drop on a trained killer and his partner when they attempted to kill me in the gas station. And earlier today that kung fu lady had dropped her guard just long enough for me to knock her silly.

There was no way in hell my luck was going to hold.

"I can't go," she said quietly.

What? "Why not?"

She didn't answer.

After a moment, I repeated the question. "Why not?"

She still didn't answer, but I understood.

"You're nothing but dead weight to me," I said firmly. "If you hang around you're just going to get me killed. I need to be able to do whatever the moment calls for and not—"

"You don't even have a *car*. You know you need me," she interrupted me. "All you have to do is turn the car back on and we can be in Florida in five hours."

Not a bad idea. But somehow I was certain that geography wasn't going to solve this problem.

"Then what?" I asked. "Are we going to change our names and live happily ever after?"

Tears welled in her eyes. I knew at that instant that she wasn't going anywhere without a shove. I took a deep breath.

"Look here, *Kermit*." My voice was cold, condescending. "Maybe you've got some misplaced little crush on me, but it ain't gonna happen. Believe me, you're not my type. You don't want to take this fancy little car of yours and fly home to Mommy and Daddy, fine. But hanging around me is just gonna get you killed. I don't care what you do, just get the *fuck* away from me. I've got enough problems already; babysitting some stupid girl is definitely gonna get me killed." I climbed out and slammed the door as an exclamation point.

I felt horrible, but I'd had no choice. If she would only get to the airport in time, she'd have the rest of her life to figure it out. Without looking back, I crossed the street to the boardwalk.

Old Stone Mountain was a collection of shops designed to give off the feel of "small-town America." These days it was more or less a tourist trap—complete with souvenirs and overpriced antique shops everywhere—but it actually had a couple decent restaurants and one really cool coffee shop.

I wasn't hungry, so I headed for the coffee shop. It was

91

tiny—only six tables—and located on top of a chocolate shop, accessible only by a narrow staircase at the back of the store. I took a seat at a table on a narrow balcony overlooking the street.

What now? What on earth could I do? Jessica was right: I didn't even have a car.

Suddenly Jessica was standing right in front of me, glaring down. "First, you are a complete *asshole*. Second, I don't have 'some little crush' on you, so don't flatter yourself."

"Um, I'll come back in a minute," said the waitress who had followed Jessica out. She quickly backed through the door.

"Third, what makes you think I'll be safe simply because we part ways? The last two times they came for you, who were you with? *Me*. So thanks to you, *I'm* probably on their list of people to kill. So I'm staying. Like it or not," Jessica said resolutely. "And now you can apologize."

I can't tell you how relieved I felt as I sat there looking up her wagging finger and angry scowl. I knew I should probably say something cruel and force her to leave, but all I wanted to do was hug her.

"Jessica, I am—"

"I know," she interrupted me, taking a chair. She reached across the table and squeezed my hand.

"I thought about the fact that they might also be looking for you," I said. "But I still think your chances are far better without me."

"I don't agree. I think the only way either one of us has any chance to survive is if we stick together."

I considered her words. I wasn't convinced, but I couldn't argue with the probability that they were looking for her as well. And if it was me they were after, what would they do with her? It was quite clear that they'd have no compunctions about snuffing her out if she served no other use.

92

She interrupted my thoughts. "Dale, this is completely nuts. What do you think was going on back there? Who was shooting at who and why? It just doesn't make sense."

"Yeah, that was crazy. Like some kind of military operation right in the middle of Atlanta. Whatever's going on, a lot of people seem to be taking it pretty seriously."

"I think we need to go straight to the police," she said.

I looked down from the balcony. Right across the street was a building with two police cruisers parked in front. The sign read "Stone Mountain Sheriff's Office."

"Seriously," Jessica continued. "I'm sure they want to talk to us about what just happened at Manuel's. Why don't we just go in, tell them that we think our professor and the others were murdered, and that people are trying to kill us. All we have to do is tell them our side of things, and then it's not our problem anymore. If these people are after you because they want to shut you up, then we should hurry up and talk before they find us. I mean, what's the point in killing us if the word is already out?"

She made a damn good point and I was ready to agree, but then the image of her sitting in the police station with that strange cop floated into my mind.

"Jessica... I think the cops are in on it," I said. "That guy you were sitting with the other night—the one who was at my accident? What if he was part of it? What if he was in on the attempt to kill me?"

Her eyes widened as the logic of this sank in.

"Listen, I know it seems like going to the police is the right thing to do, but that guy... there's no way he just *happened* to be driving along behind me at the very moment I was supposed to be killed in a car 'accident.' I don't trust taking our chances with the police," I said. "But you're right. We do have to *do* something. So far we've just been victims, sitting ducks. If we keep running, they *will* catch us eventually."

"Okay, then what do we do?"

"The best defense is often a good offense."

Her brow furrowed as she waited for more. I shrugged. That was all I had.

"Yeah, and a bird in the hand is better than two in the bush," she said sarcastically. "Maybe we can beat them to death with clichés?"

The waitress returned, and seemed relieved to see that we were no longer arguing. I ordered a coffee, Jessica a tea. Nowhere else to go—this balcony was as good as the next place—so we might as well make ourselves comfortable while we figured out our next step.

I considered what Jessica had said. She was right: the only logical reason why anyone would want to kill me would be to shut me up. More and more I was starting to like her idea of simply getting the word out.

"Why do they call me Kermit?" Jessica asked quietly.

Well, that was unexpected. I looked up to find her staring sadly into her tea. Shit.

"Listen, it's really not that bad," I said. "I have a friend that everybody calls Pee-Pee Man. I've known him for like five years and I have no clue what his real name is. One night, forever and a day ago, he got so drunk that he pissed his pants at a party. That one incident stuck with him—and as much as he hates it, it'll be with him forever."

She looked me right in the eyes. "Can you please just answer the question?"

There was no ducking. It really wasn't that big of a deal.

"It's just jealousy," I said. "Because you always get good grades, because you never really hang out with everybody, because you're kind of a teacher's pet."

"Answer the question, asshole."

"Oh, for crying out loud, it's because you're so uptight and self-righteous. Somebody said your ass was probably

94

as watertight as a frog, and next thing you know they were calling you Kermit."

Jessica was back to studying her tea. Then, halfheartedly, she said: "So, how can we go on the offense?"

"Look, you're making a federal case out of nothing." I said, refusing to let her change the subject again. "Being called Kermit has to be a hell of a lot better than if they called you Miss Piggy."

She was quiet for a moment. "Do *you* call me Kermit?"

"Oh, come on," I said, exasperated. Fine. I wasn't much for beating around the bush anyway. "Yes, probably. I never really gave it much thought. I didn't really know you. I don't think anybody ever meant it to be mean. It just seemed to fit."

"So you think I'm 'uptight'?" she asked. I caught a glimpse of sly humor in her eyes and realized that the pouty expression was fake.

"If the shoe fits," I grinned. "Seriously, have you ever gotten a B on anything in your life?"

"Whatever." The humor disappeared from her eyes. I could almost see her thoughts returning to our situation.

"Listen, I've been thinking," I said. "I really like your idea of just telling people what's going on. Why don't we go back to my apartment? There are bound to be reporters camped out all over the place."

"Uh... I don't think that's such a good idea."

"Why not?"

"Hello? Go back to where you live? These guys seem to be over the whole 'let's kill him but try not to make it look like murder' thing. I bet they're waiting inside your apartment, hoping you're dumb enough to go home. Better yet, they're outside, posing as reporters. The moment you start talking, bang."

She had a good point.

"Do you know any reporters?" I asked.

She gave me a look that said *yeah, right*.

That's when I hit gold. If only we could manage to survive long enough. But I had an idea for that, too.

"Let's get out of here—I have an idea."

We were making our way through the dining area when Jessica caught my hand. I drew up, and she nodded toward a TV behind the counter. It was on mute, but I didn't have to hear what they were saying. The screen was showing the carnage outside Manuel's Tavern.

When the image changed to yearbook pictures of Jessica and me, the waitress gasped, and we were out the door.

Chapter 9
HOMECOMING

What is it about times of trouble that send a person home? No matter how far you've come, no matter how much you think you've changed—as soon as the shit hits the fan all pretense is forgotten.

Home for me was not an apartment in Decatur. And family was not the yuppie larvae I had been running around with for the last few years at Emory. Home was Doraville, and family was the guys from the neighborhood.

I was not a very good brother. When my mom passed, the first thing I did was to get out of the neighborhood. I had been accepted into Emory, but couldn't afford to live on campus, so I ended up in Decatur.

Most of my buddies weren't exactly college material. Several of them had done a spin or two behind bars. One had gotten murdered a few months after I left. Little Mikey had taken a job at the GM plant. Far as I know, he and I were the only two to get out.

As much as I loved the friends I grew up with, I had wanted to get as far away from Doraville as possible. Unfortunately, this had meant turning my back on the old neighborhood.

But now, in a time of crisis, that's exactly where I turned for refuge.

The Atlanta Rhythm Section once described Doraville as "a touch of country in the city." But when our generation replaced theirs, rednecks drinking wine on the porch were replaced by a more desperate element.

Doraville didn't have quite the violent reputation of some of the most notorious areas in Atlanta, such as the old Techwood Homes. Despite this lack of notoriety, the kids who grew up there got to see more than their share of Atlanta's underbelly. Within all of the Atlanta metro area, one of the highest concentrations of homicides occurs within a few blocks of Buford Highway, on a two-mile stretch starting about a mile inside the perimeter and running one mile out—cutting right through Doraville. This violence is attributed in no small part to the gangs that prey on illegals who don't use banks. Pockets stuffed with cashed paychecks make inviting targets on a Friday night.

Though the rest of Atlanta never paid attention—unless they were hungry—Doraville was the kind of town that evoked quite a bit of emotion in those of us who grew up there.

Maybe it's due to its unfortunate geography? It's one thing to be poor and grow up in a tough neighborhood. Life in general sucks for poor kids. But the kids who grew up poor in Doraville—due to the way somebody drew lines on a map—also ended up going to high school with some of the wealthiest kids in Atlanta.

Doraville borders on Dunwoody, so every day we all piled onto buses, crossed over Peachtree Industrial, and went to school at Peachtree High in Dunwoody. And with Doraville kids making up less than ten percent of the student population... well, we pretty much stuck together.

Maybe I'm making it sound worse than it actually was. Yeah, there was a lot of fighting early on, and it sucked having your locker turned out every couple weeks. But, by the end of it all, we pretty much ran things. Everybody knew who threw the best parties.

For me, the worst part of going to school in Dunwoody was the ride home. The bus would cut through nice suburban neighborhoods, letting kids off here and there in front of big, beautiful homes, meticulously manicured lawns, and June Cleaver waiting with open arms for little Beav to run in. And then we'd take a right on Tilly Mill and cross Peachtree... where the suburban fairy tale suddenly gave way to a series of two-bedroom, one-bath hovels, overgrown yards with cars on blocks, and fat drunk guys sitting on the porch in stained T-shirts, ready to chunk a beer can at little Jimmy. Somehow I doubted the Dunwoody kids listened to their redneck neighbors' nightly screaming matches. And nobody ever got stabbed or shot under the streetlights of a Dunwoody neighborhood.

Dusk had fallen by the time Jessica and I hit Buford Highway. Signs on both sides of the road were well lit, but the lighting did little to make them legible. Most of what could be read was in Spanish, and the rest was just Asian hieroglyphs. If you knew where to look, Buford Highway had some of the best ethnic food in North America.

I hung a right between a triple-X theater and a liquor store, then another quick right into a neighborhood behind the theater.

"Are you lost?" Jessica asked nervously.

"No, don't worry, I know this neighborhood," I answered.

A car in front of us stopped short, and an Asian kid with sagging pants crossed the street to the driver's window. It didn't take a rocket scientist to see what was going on.

Before I could pull around, another kid was at my door. I recognized him even before he rapped on the window.

"Oh, shit," he exclaimed, as he recognized me, too.

"Giggles, what the fuck are you doing out here?" I asked.

"Oh man, you know, nothin'… just talking to folks and shit…" He trailed off, looking at Jessica uncertainly.

"You need to take your little butt home. Does your brother know you're out here? How old are you?"

"He's over at Clyde's. They said you'd be coming." He smiled. "I'm fifteen."

"Whatever," I told the little liar as I pulled away. How did they know I was coming?

"I don't like this," said Jessica.

"Me either." I smiled sadly. "This is why God invented Emory."

A short way down the street, I pulled up in front of Clyde's house. There were a couple of cars in the driveway and a handful of folks sitting on the porch. I didn't recognize anybody except Jorge, who hopped up as soon as I stepped out of the car.

"Oh shit, Books!" Jorge came down the steps as we approached. He grabbed me in a bear hug.

Jorge was a big guy—though more in terms of girth than height. He was only five-ten, but he must've weighed in at around three-twenty. I used to love going to parties with him when we were in high school because he had pretty much always looked exactly as he did now: like a big, fat, badass Puerto Rican gangster.

Yes, Doraville is thick with gangs, but none of my good friends were bangers. In fact, even Jorge was no gang member, though he professed to be "affiliated," as they say, with God knows who.

Jorge moved into Doraville from Los Angeles when we were kids. He was always talking shit about gangs before any of us even thought about that kind of thing. And slowly he sort of transformed to match his words.

He was the first of us to sprout facial hair and the first to get a tattoo. Believe me, he scared the hell out of milquetoast

100

students and faculty at Peachtree. He grew a goatee and shaved his head, added some facial piercings, and walked around school with sagging pants and the word "KEMO" tattooed on his neck so the whole world could see it. It didn't take long before they ran him out.

And Jorge had a big mouth. Whenever he wanted to impress folks with how tough he was, he would use a lot of Spanglish. But in truth, he never actually got into fights, and he was for the most part pretty harmless.

Nonetheless, Mr. Walker, the discipline administrator, found an excuse to boot Jorge out in the tenth grade. Jorge and another kid, Anthony, had been making a little money by doing yard work in Dunwoody on the weekends. Unfortunately, Jorge had forgotten to take his tools out of the car before driving it to school… and one of those tools was a machete.

It was actually kind of sad what happened to him. Though he'd never admit it, I'm pretty sure ol' Jorge is illiterate in two languages. And although his gang talk had started out as hot air, he quickly began rolling with the real deal. Two guys he brought to one of our parties got murdered in a crack house off Shallowford the following weekend.

Anyway, he was fun to roll with for the intimidation factor. Right after he caught the boot from school, he added two new tattoos: a ring of flames around the thick of his forearm, one on each arm, to give the appearance of flaming fists. He very much looked the part of a serious OG. When we showed up at a party in Dunwoody or Henderson or Tucker… well, we rarely got hassled. As long as he kept his mouth shut, nobody realized he was just a big goofy pussycat.

"Get off me," I pushed him away. "What the fuck are you doing, turning Giggles out like that? Man, the neighborhood looks like a dope spot."

"Relax, bro. It's just a little weed. Ain't like he's slingin' rock and shit," he said, as if that somehow made it all good. He turned his attention to Jessica. "You must be the Jessica we've heard so much about."

"Yes," she answered, looking at me quizzically. Since I hadn't talked to anybody over here in at least two years, I was as clueless as she was.

"Clyde said to take your cell phones and car keys."

"What?" I looked at him irritably. "Don't be weird, man. Where's Clyde?"

"I'm serious, Books. Give me your shit or get the fuck out of here. We know you're on the run. That's the only reason you'd come home."

My ears stung from the undisguised disgust in his voice.

"They're looking for your car, dumbass. What's it gonna be?"

That made sense. And I hadn't thought about the traceability of cell phones. Jessica held up her keys.

"What are you going to do with my car?"

"Does it matter?" Jorge asked flatly.

One of the guys on the porch came down and took our things from Jorge. Another walked around to the back of the car with a screwdriver and busied himself switching out the license plate. They were climbing into the vehicle as we entered the house.

There was a card game going on in the kitchen, beer on the table, smoke thick in the air. But it was oddly quiet and the mood didn't seem to fit a laid-back game. I was surprised to see little Mikey at the table.

"Gee guys, look who's slumming tonight. It's our old pal Books," said Clyde, discarding. His back was to us and he didn't bother to turn around.

"What is this, a family reunion? Josh, Jorge, Clyde... even little Mikey. Thought you moved away, Mikey," I said. "What's Clyde's problem?"

Mikey smiled. "Yeah, I don't get around much. Wife, kid, work. You know…"

"You gonna discard or run your fucking mouth all night?" Clyde growled at Mikey.

"Chill out, asshole," returned Mike, discarding.

Clyde still hadn't turned around, but suddenly his chair kicked back violently. Maybe it was my tired, sore body, or maybe it was the surprise factor. Whatever the excuse, Clyde had the better of me in a split second and the next thing you know I was on the ground getting wailed on. What the hell?

The table was overturned, and cards and drinks went flying everywhere as people rushed to pull him off of me. Then I was showered in beer and glass as a bottle was smashed over his head.

It was weird, like somebody turned off the music on a dance floor or something. The bottle smashing on his head was so unexpected that everybody just stopped in their tracks. We were even more shocked to realize that it was the very pretty, very petite Jessica who was backing away and holding the top portion of the broken bottle like a knife.

The moment hung in the air for a second. Clyde was frozen in place with a balled fist in the air, ready to strike me again. He stared up at her in confusion.

"Jesus Christ!" he bellowed, coming to his senses and climbing off of me. "What the fuck did you do that for, stupid bitch?"

"Watch your fucking mouth!" I yelled, lunging off the floor.

I caught him about the midsection and drove him up onto the counter, spilling dishes, bottles, and whatever else onto the floor. We struggled briefly before they pulled us apart.

"Let me go!" Jessica was fighting to get away from Jorge. He had disarmed her and was attempting to restrain her with a big grin on his face. Then she bit his arm.

103

"Oh my God, she's crazy!"

Once again, she'd turned the music off. We all just stared at her.

"Jorge, you should know better than to be grabbing on chicks." I laughed.

Calm returned. Clyde and I were released. My nose was bleeding again, running down my chin. Somebody handed me a dirty dishtowel.

"Clyde, what the hell was that?" I demanded, wiping my face with the dishtowel. "I didn't do shit, man. I haven't even seen you in forever. What the hell are you so mad about?"

"Fuck you," he growled, straightening out his clothes.

"It's because I don't come around anymore?"

"What are you, retarded? I could care less about that," he scoffed.

"Dude, none of us would come around if we had anyplace better to be," interjected Jorge. "Man, everybody was proud of you going to school and shit. We thought you were doing great. Then we find out you're out robbing banks and killing cops."

"Robbing *what?*" I shouted, completely flabbergasted.

"Whatever man, no point in acting all surprised. It's all over the news. My mom even knows about it," Clyde said with disgust.

"We heard about the gas station last night. They *were* calling you a hero because nobody knew the truth," said Mike. "But your little shootout downtown today is all over the news now—"

"I saw your picture on CNN," Josh added.

"—and they're saying the police linked your fingerprints to a string of bank robberies," finished Mike. "So Clyde is right, no point in lying about it."

"I can't believe you killed a fucking cop." Clyde was shaking his head. "You know they're gonna give you the

104

death penalty for that. We're probably *all* gonna do time, just because your dumb ass is here."

I felt like somebody had thrown me over a cliff. I couldn't wrap my mind around it. I remembered the police taking my fingerprints, but that was just to screen me out of the crime scene at the gas station. How could my fingerprints be linked to a bank robbery?

Jessica was staring at me numbly.

I finally found my voice. "Look, they're framing me. I swear."

"Whatever, bro," said Jorge.

"I never even touched a gun today, let alone shoot some cop."

"Come on, they're showing surveillance footage of you running around in that gas station with a shotgun. I saw you with my own eyes, pendejo," said Jorge.

"Wait, that was different. That was different. It *was* me in the gas station. But I took the gun from some dude that was robbing the place. It wasn't my gun. I swear!"

"And the footage of you and Jessica robbing a bank? Your mom is probably rolling over in her grave."

Now it was Jessica's turn to be shocked. "What? *Me?*"

"What makes you think it was us?" I asked.

"Well, you were wearing masks," said Jorge. "But the cops said your fingerprints were all over the place."

I looked around the room. Nobody was happy with me. Everybody seemed to believe this nonsense. And these were my friends!

"Listen, you guys have to believe me. I swear to God, I never robbed any bank," I said sincerely. Looking around at the accusing eyes, I could see no one was impressed by my oath. "Just let me explain. You're not going to believe this."

For the next half hour I talked, with Jessica adding things here and there, and they listened. It was a wild story and I might not have believed it myself if I wasn't actually living it. But these guys had known me forever and could tell I wasn't lying. In the end, I was absolved in their eyes.

"So you two aren't *together* together then?" asked Jorge with a mischievous grin.

"Calm down, Jorge. She's not into fat Mexicans." I laughed.

"Fuck you, you know I'm Puerto Rican," he snapped.

I've always been mystified by the fact that one of the greatest insults to a non-Mexican Hispanic is to call them Mexican. You can mistake a Mexican for a Puerto Rican and he'll simply correct you. But call a Puerto Rican or Cuban a Mexican and you're liable to have your head torn off.

Jorge recovered quickly, smiling at Jessica. "Don't listen to him, baby. There's just more of me to love."

"So who were those people at the bar? It almost sounds like they were trying to help you," Clyde said, coming out of deep thought.

"Yeah, I don't know," I scratched my head. "I've been thinking about that. Even before the police showed up, people were shooting at people. If those guys wanted us dead, they could have just shot us while we were sitting at the table."

"Seems like there are three groups that want us," Jessica pointed out. "Whoever killed the professor, the people from the bar, and now the police."

"Think this is what you call Shit Stew," quipped Jorge.

"Thanks for your analysis. Eloquent as usual," I said, shaking my head. "But, yeah, I agree. There do seem to be three groups." I paused. "Actually, maybe it's just two. I think the cops are working with whoever's doing the killing. Jessica asked the lady at Manuel's Tavern if she was a cop. She said no."

"That's not exactly right," she corrected me. "What I asked was if she was with the FBI."

"In any event, it almost sounds like they were there to keep somebody else from killing you," Clyde said. "Books, I think you screwed up big time by running from them."

Jessica rose to my defense. "How were we supposed to know? It's not like people were wearing jerseys that read 'Good Guy' or 'Bad Guy.'"

"Okay, so we know that there are at least two groups looking for you," Clyde said. "One clearly wants you dead, and the other group may or may not want you dead. And we know that this all has to do with your gravity thing. We're not sure what these mystery people want, but we know that the guys who want you dead are trying to shut you up."

"Sounds about right," I agreed.

"Well, who cares what the mystery people want? We pop 'em all and ask questions later," Jorge stated matter-of-factly, tugging at a piece tucked in his waistband.

"Great idea, smart guy," I said. "Tell me, Jorge, who do we kill first?"

Jorge replied without hesitation. "The Georgia Green Bean guy. Conservation my ass! I bet he's like a double agent or something. He's the one we have to kill."

We were all amazed. For once something Jorge said actually made sense. It had to be Simmons from the Greener Georgia Initiative. His bio listed an impressive resume, with stints as an executive at various energy corporations before taking his philanthropic position at Greener Georgia. He had to be very well connected. And I was willing to bet his loyalty was with the money.

"Dale, tell them your plan," Jessica said nervously. She didn't know Jorge well enough to realize he was full of shit.

"Yeah. Listen, no need to 'cap' anybody, Jorge," I said sarcastically. "All we have to do is survive long enough to get the word out, put some simple do-it-yourself videos online, and they'll have no—"

"Wait," said Clyde. "That guy you shot in the gas station. Didn't you say somebody paid millions to bail that dude out?"

"Yes."

Clyde smiled thoughtfully. "And you figure the reason somebody would pay millions to have you killed would be to prevent this gravity thing from getting out. How much do you think this thing is worth?"

I didn't like the glint in his eye. "A bunch."

I was intentionally vague. But Clyde wasn't stupid. He persisted. "Millions?"

No point in fighting whatever evil seed was sprouting. "Okay, yeah, probably."

A sly grin crept across Clyde's face.

"Hell yeah, baby," shouted Jorge, slapping my back so hard I almost fell over. "We're rich! Oh my God, I told you! I tell everybody about you: my buddy Books, he goes to Emory. He's smart as shit, you watch—he's gonna be a big pimp in a suit. I knew it! You wouldn't forget us. See, he saves the good shit for us!"

"Shut your yap," Clyde said quietly, still staring at me with that sly look. Slowly he turned his attention back to Jorge. "In case you were sleeping earlier, half the world thinks these two are a couple of cop-killing bank robbers, and the other half is trying to kill them. I'm pretty sure Books ain't got a million bucks in his back pocket."

Wow, that was actually pretty rational of Clyde. Usually when he gets that look...

"So here's the plan," I continued. "All I need—"

Clyde interrupted me again. "How many millions? Two? Twenty? Two hundred?"

"Maybe. But it doesn't really matter," I said carefully. "Clyde, I know you're thinking about money. But believe me, these guys are no joke. Ask Jessica—that little shootout on Highland today was like some shit straight off the streets of

108

Baghdad. All I want to do is survive long enough to pick up my diploma. Screw money."

Clyde was quiet for a moment. Jorge had a great big dopey look on his face. If he were a dog, he would've been panting and his tail would've been wagging like mad. He was on Clyde's side, no matter what Clyde's side was.

"So would you say this thing is a million-dollar idea?" Clyde asked quietly.

I looked at Jessica. She shrugged.

"Yeah," I said.

"Would you say that this thing is a billion-dollar idea?"

Though the truth was as plain as the nose on my face, I had a harder time answering. Finally, "Yes. Maybe. I don't know. Probably."

"Hmm, okay. Can you remind me again about your *other* billion-dollar idea?"

"What other idea?"

"That's what I thought." He smiled. "How about telling us about one of your million-dollar ideas?"

I didn't bother answering. He continued, "Oh, gee. I'm sorry, I forgot. You don't have any other big-money ideas. Maybe we should go with one of Jorge's great ideas."

I was quiet for a moment, trying to think my way out of this conversation.

Jorge shrugged. "I always wanted to open a Kentucky Fried Chicken."

Clyde shook his head slowly. "Are you feeling me, man?"

"I get it. It's a big deal."

"No, you don't get it," Clyde shot back, shaking his head with frustration. "This is a *once-in-a-lifetime* big deal. Bro, you just won the lottery of big ideas. And now you want to give it away just because somebody took a few shots at you?"

"Okay, so what do *you* think we should do?" Jessica asked Clyde.

"Blackmail 'em." He grinned.

"Blackmail who? We don't even know for sure who *they* are," I pointed out.

"I think Jorge is right, it has to be Simons," said Jessica. "He's the guy we have to go after."

"Go *after*? Are you crazy? Don't tell me you're buying into this."

I couldn't believe it. I looked around the room. It was clear I was alone.

I spent the next half hour on the losing side of the debate. Even Jessica was firmly on Clyde's side. What finally turned me had less to do with the greed that motivated Clyde and Jorge and more to do with recognizing the sheer scope of powerful forces that had been arrayed against me.

If the situation had been simpler, I would never have given up my fight against this insane plan to somehow extort money from God knows who. But my enemies clearly had power—a *lot* of power—and were exercising it on two devastating fronts. On one front, they were trying to kill me. On the other, they were framing me for robbery and murder. Murder of police officers, no less.

Even if I somehow survived their attempts to kill me long enough to get my idea out to the public, who was to say that these guys would *stop* trying to kill me? And if they did stop, these bullshit allegations against me would probably send me to prison for the rest of my life. Jorge's description of Shit Stew was, in fact, fairly apt.

They'd boxed me in. All "reasonable" courses of action would almost surely lead directly to my death or detainment.

Faced with a choice between bad and worse, I could think of only one way to possibly get my life back.

Rip it out of their fucking jaws.

Chapter 10
BUS STOP

"**P**lease tell me you're joking," I said, closing my eyes and wishing it away. "This thing is just begging to get pulled over. Can't we take *your* car, Clyde?"

"In the shop," Clyde replied simply, opening the passenger door for Jessica.

Jorge grinned at me through the open window. His chariot was a deep maroon '75 Chevy Nova, complete with lift kit and widened wheel wells to accommodate forty-four-inch black rims. The mural of a mostly nude Spanish goddess lying in a bed of flowers classed up the side of the vehicle.

I noticed Jorge had tied a bandanna around his head. "What are you supposed to be, a Mexican Tupac?"

His grin was instantly wiped. He gunned the engine, glass-packed mufflers roaring. Jorge growled at me: "Get your puto ass in the car, ese."

I felt a little guilty as I rounded the vehicle. Jorge was proud of his ride. Clyde was holding the door. I tossed my duffel bag on the floorboard, climbed up, and slid in next to Jessica.

Jessica started to say something, but the noisy car leaped forward. In the same instant Jorge flipped on his sound system, the deep bass punching my lungs and rattling the windows. Clyde spent a very animated twenty seconds yelling something no one could hear, then punched Jorge hard.

Jorge cut the music way down, ignoring the pain. "Yo man, I got twin twelves and a bazooka box—"

"Yeah man, I could feel it. Think you broke my ribs, bro." I laughed, popping him on the shoulder. "What you got pushing it?"

"Nobody cares about your ghetto-ass sound system," Clyde interrupted. He leaned back, handing me a gun, butt first. I hesitated. "Take it man, it's good. Cleaned it yesterday. Shoots straight."

I took it and put it in my bag. He stared at me for a moment, then turned back.

We rode in silence. Outkast's *Spaghetti Junction* played in the background as we hit I-85, southbound toward town.

Jessica was lost in her own world. I marveled at her from across the chasm. She seemed so calm, knees crossed, delicate hands folded in her lap, casually dressed in a cashmere blouse and capris. She could just as easily be weekending in the Hamptons.

Refined. Dignified. A true lady. How had I never noticed how impossibly large her eyes were?

Yet here she was, rolling with a two-bit gangster, a knuckle-busting thug, and a con artist.

Con. That's what you do when you don't belong anywhere but you have to fit everywhere. I've spent my life passing myself off as different things to different people. In high school I got into advanced classes, tried to keep pace with the smart kids, and managed not to get found out. I spent my weekends getting high and joyriding in boosted cars, and nobody there figured me out. Spent Sundays and Wednesdays with Bible thumpers at my mom's church, and never got struck by lightning. Spent the last few years listening to rich kids talk about cutting freshies in Aspen over break—while avoiding questions about my own holidays—and nobody gave me a second thought.

Don't ask, don't tell. Keep your head down. Don't lie—just keep them talking about themselves and pretty soon they'll see their reflection. It's easy to be liked that way: people love themselves.

But I could never shake the feeling that I was an imposter. One misplaced word away from being found out.

I felt very hollow as I studied Jessica's resolute eyes. Our situation was absurdly out of control, but she seemed so serene. If she only knew in whom she had placed her trust.

God, I hope I don't get her killed.

Jessica turned and caught me looking at her. She smiled at my attempt to look away and pretend I hadn't been staring.

Jorge took us right through the heart of the Five Points and Highlands areas, where all the chaos had so recently occurred. A flashlight-waving policeman directed us around a detour that sealed off the area surrounding Manuel's Tavern. I hunkered down, but there was no way for the cop to see us through the silver-tinted windows.

A quarter mile away, Jorge took a left on Samson Street, rolling slowly down an industrial block. Hookers and hustlers dotted the street. A few blocks down, several large men wearing rolled-up jeans over combat boots stood under a light in front of an old brick warehouse. I could see the yellow word *SECURITY* on the back of two them. Just beyond them was a line, three people deep, stretching off into distant shadows.

"Cut down the first driveway," Clyde said.

Just before reaching the security guards, Jorge hooked left down a gravel driveway between two brick buildings. When he turned right at the back, his headlights shone on a wide-loaded tractor-trailer with half a house on it.

"Hi honey, we're home." Jorge laughed as he parked in front of the Peterbilt.

We climbed out and found that the night air had a bit of a nip. The back of the warehouse had two docks and a rusted staircase leading up to a door on the far side. A rapid, muffled thud could be heard through the wall: techno.

Clyde led us up the steps and banged his fist on the heavy steel door. A light above the door flicked on briefly, and I looked up at a video camera. A crooked, peeling sticker on the door read *BUS STOP*. A short wait, then loud clanking as the door was unbolted. When the door opened, a blast of music seemed to shove a meaty skinhead out onto the landing.

"Clyde, what up, man?" the skinhead said, extending a beefy paw. He wore a blue security T-shirt and his arms were densely inked all the way to the wrists. He eyed Jorge, and the butt tucked in Jorge's waistband, with less enthusiasm. "'S'up, Kemo?"

Jorge ignored the offered fist bump as he pushed past. As I entered, a glimpse of the man's neck helped me understand the issue. Tattooed on his neck beside a confederate flag were three thick, black letters: *OGS*.

In Atlanta, "skinhead" doesn't necessarily translate to "hate." In fact, Skinheads Against Fascist Tendencies, better known as SHAFT, was a group that devoted their noisy angst to hunting racist skins. The word "skinhead" seemed to be more about music and lifestyle. While catching an underground band like Bad Brains at the Masquerade, it was not unusual to bump into a black skinhead.

Yes, as unlikely as that sounds, there are indeed black skinheads. There's no other name for a baldheaded, shit-kicking, black punk in a white T-shirt, suspenders, rolled-up jeans, and ten-hole oxblood Doc Martens. We used to call them ska skins because large groups of them would turn up

114

for ska shows. Ska, for the uninitiated, was born in Jamaica as a fusion of calypso and jazz, a precursor to reggae. It was adopted by British mods in the sixties, and later bastardized by the punk rock scene. If Sid Vicious and Peter Tosh had had sex while listening to Dizzy Gillespie, the baby's name would have been Ska.

But OGS, or Old Glory Skin, was a particularly nasty bunch of preachy racists. Three or four of them had jumped a buddy of ours—Billy, a quiet white kid who never bothered anybody—outside a Fellini's Pizza. Pounded him senseless with brass knuckles, leaving him in the hospital for a month. For no reason other than they just felt like it.

So Jorge's animosity toward the racist prick was understandable. Clyde being cool with this douchebag was another matter.

As we stepped into the dimly lit, narrow hallway, I saw men coming and going quickly from a door on the right, and a line of women waiting to get in another door farther down. Beyond them, the hall opened into a cavern packed with people. Their existence came through in black and white flashes, the silhouettes in a different position every time a strobe light popped.

Nobody paid any attention to us. Clyde rapped on the only door on the left wall. I followed his gaze to a camera above the door. The door buzzed, and we went in.

The room was large and open—it was maybe forty feet up to the ceiling—and the cement floor had been disguised by a layer of hardwood. We stood near three couches arranged around a sixty-inch flatscreen; jumbled in a cabinet beneath the TV were a dozen electronic devices, including several game consoles. To our left was a granite-topped island surrounded by tall stools and an open kitchen. In the far back corner a black steel staircase led up to an open loft with a bed.

When Jorge closed the door behind us, the room was

115

surprisingly quiet. Soundproofing.

My attention was immediately drawn to a figure in the far front corner, sitting at a large desk, surrounded by four computer monitors.

"Aaaah, shit! Doraville boys unite! What it is, Books!" he called out, pushing out of the chair and practically running across the room.

"'S'up, Flip." I smiled, returning the man-hug. "This is my friend, Jessica. Jessica, this is Flip, the world's biggest brain."

"It's true. Almost twice as big as his." Flip laughed, hugging Jessica as well. "Any friend of Books is a friend of mine." Flip took a moment to examine my face, now that he was close. "Damn, son, you look like something the dog been chewin'."

Flip was modded out. Tall, skinny, close-cropped red hair; checkered vans, tight orange pants, a too-small T-shirt that said *RIOT*, and plain, black-rimmed glasses. His real name was Phil Sibley, but I had known him my whole life as Flip.

"What's up with the OGS clowns you got working the doors?" I asked.

"Ah, man, that's just business. They keep the peace around here. Even Kemo's cool with it."

Jorge shrugged.

"Since when do you make decisions based on what Jorge thinks?"

"Hey man, bite me. Look at this shit," Flip fired back, pulling aside a huge length of curtain on the front wall.

The curtains had been covering a twenty-foot-long tinted one-way window. Flashes of light revealed a sea of heads bouncing up and down in unison.

"Twenty bucks a pop to get in. On a good night it's five thousand heads. You do the math, man. At that table alone I'll pull down more than enough to cover all my overhead," Flip said, indicating a table off to the left where a woman was

116

collecting money and handing out balloons. Nitrous oxide. "Plus I *print* money at the smart bar over on the other side. And usually Clyde is out there working the crowd. I get a nice taste of that action, too."

I looked at Clyde; he shrugged. "Mostly X. And some A. I've got a pretty good connection for party favors. Pick it up in bulk for next to nothing. Lab is local. He's right, we're making bank."

"It's a business, brother," Flip continued. "I do this shit once a month."

"What about the cops?" I asked.

"Fuck 'em, they don't care. Long as I grease a few beat cops, everybody's happy. I live here. Far as they're concerned, I'm just a dude with a lot of friends that likes to throw big-ass parties. Everybody's making money. Kelner keeps his OGS boys in check, they step on trouble before it starts and keep the locals away." Flip paused, looking at Jessica. "Besides, it's good theater. Half the crowd out there are from the 'burbs. They get off on the whole edgy underground thing, dig having big scary skinheads working the doors. I've been thinking about raising the price to fifty bucks a head for anybody with Gwinnett on their license plate."

Flip laughed. Outside the window, the strobe lights had stopped. It was very dark, except for the glowsticks that dotted the room. Suddenly the lights came up again and the crowd went wild.

"You live here?" Jessica asked, cringing at the thought.

Flip chuckled at her disdain. "Yup, this is home sweet home, baby. The 'hood is a bit darker than Doraville, but being a Doraville boy makes me an honorary brother." He smiled at her. "That's the Cavern," he said, pointing to the great room on the other side of the window. Then he waived at the living quarters that surrounded us. "And this the Crib. Makes for a short commute to the ole office."

Flip's attention returned to me. "Books," he said with a disappointed sigh. "You're the last person I expected would be talkin' smack about the people I run with. You with your little one-percenter glee club over at Emory." He laughed again. Then, looking at Jessica, he added: "No offense, sweetheart."

"Whatever," I snapped. "I thought you were off changing the world at MIT?"

Flip studied me hard, trying to figure out what I knew. Finally he said, "Boston is a cool town and all, but ain't no place like the A. Cambridge is hell on a Doraville boy."

I knew a story was there, but I let it slide. "Thanks for putting us up, man."

"So Clyde says all this crazy stuff on the news is over some skateboard? Where is it? I want to see it."

"I'm pretty sure it's not just about a skateboard," I said, sitting down on a couch and digging through my duffel bag. "More about how it works."

I set my skateboard on the glass coffee table in front of me. Everybody gathered in for a closer look. I reached out and hit the red button.

After a long silence, Jessica was the first to speak. "Wow. I mean, I knew it was real… I saw the video. But seeing it in front of me… Wow. It looks so… it's like an optical illusion or something."

She reached out and poked the board, and it glided toward Flip, who steadied it with his hand on top. Looking up at me, Flip asked: "Can I try it? Can I take it for a spin?"

"Go ahead."

Flip pushed it off the table, and it floated down to hover six inches off the ground. He looked up and grinned. "That was cool!"

"Dude, that's nothing. Take it for ride, man," I said with a smile. If anybody could appreciate this experience, it was Flip. He and I had put many miles on our boards as kids.

Flip put his right foot on the board to steady it for a moment, then kicked off. He rode slowly for about forty feet, leaning in different directions to test how it handled. Right before the wall he leaned into a sharp turn and kicked off hard. Two more hard kicks and he flew past us, screaming.

He slammed into the wall so hard it just *had* to hurt. But despite his obvious agony, we were all laughing. I caught my breath long enough to say, "No brakes!"

Flip lay there, staring at the rafters. Just when I thought maybe he was really hurt, he leaped up and shouted, "*Awesome!* This thing is *unreal*. Rides so smooth, it's like butter! Unreal. Cuts really tight—as soon as you lean it changes direction. But I think I like that. Did you see how tight I cut it when I turned back?"

Without waiting for an answer, Flip was off again. And then again. And again. We all settled into the couches and just watched as Flip played with the board for the next twenty minutes.

Chapter 11
ATOMIC LOVE

Eventually Flip glided over, hopped off, and returned the board to the table. "Okay, so how does it work?" I hit the red button, and the board clattered to the table.

"To be honest, I don't really know," I answered, scratching my head. "The only thing I can get it to work with is aluminum. I can tell aluminum to attract or repel."

"So it's like the poles of a magnet?" Flip asked.

"Yeah, I guess. But I think it's more like messing with gravity itself: turning it on or off or reversing the effects of gravity with a button. I've been doing a lot of reading over the last couple weeks about the differences between gravity and magnetism. Gravity is the attractive force between all matter, but they say magnetism is nothing more than a quirky relationship caused by charged particles. Pretty much everything I've read agrees that they're two totally different things. But I'm beginning to think it's all the same song; only magnets sing in a different language and at a higher volume."

"Song?"

"Wait, let me back up. Okay, you know that the Earth travels around the sun, and the moon travels around the Earth in a perfect little pattern that can be predicted with math. Well, how the hell does the Earth know the sun is out there and that it should be attracted? Or how does the moon know we're here, we're closer, and that it shouldn't just fly off into the sun?"

I paused and looked around, then answered my own question: "They're communicating, man. They're singing little love songs to each other."

They stared at me blankly. Jorge piped up: "I want some of what you're smoking."

"Seriously man, it's a song. Check it out. Okay, imagine there's a lonely little atom floating out in space, totally bored, singing to itself. But it only knows one song and it goes like this: 'Laaaaa.'"

"Then along comes another little atom singing to itself: 'Laaaaa.' Off in the distance the first one replies: 'Laaaaa.' They fall in love and start moving toward each other. Now it's two little voices, singing the same song, only a bit louder. Another little atom hears it and falls in love—"

"Oh snap. Ménage à three, they gonna get it on!" Jorge said. "But you better change this shit up, I ain't down with three Adams. Gimme three Eves and some baby oil, yo. *Then* we in bidness."

I ignored him and continued. "So with each new atom, the song gets a bit louder. Now, atoms even farther away can hear it and come to join. Eventually enough atoms gather to form the Earth and it's singing a really beautiful love song, loud enough that the moon can hear it from two hundred and thirty thousand miles away, out in space."

"All right, that's kind of cool. I get it. So what does this have to do with magnets?" asked Clyde.

"There are two big differences between gravity and magnetism. First, gravity isn't specific. With gravity, *any* two objects that have mass are attracted to each other. But the force of magnetism is *very* specific. If you put a magnet on the side of a fridge, magnetism takes over, and it sticks. But what happens if you put a magnet on the side of a cardboard box? It won't stick. Gravity takes over and pulls the magnet to the ground. Magnets dig certain specific types of material, while gravity is just 'free love for all.'

"The other big difference is the idea of poles. If you hold two magnets close together in the right way, they'll snap together and bond tightly. But if you flip one of them over, instead of attracting, they'll repel one another—even if you try to force it. This is because *opposite* magnetic poles attract, while *like* poles resist.

"But there *is* no opposite to gravity. It has a name—levity —but science doesn't too waste much time on the opposite of gravity because it's hard to quantify something that you can't model."

Jorge was done with this conversation. He reached over, hit the red button, and pushed the board off the table. "Can I give it a go?"

"That thing ain't gonna hold your fat ass," Clyde laughed.

Jorge flipped Clyde the bird as he pushed off, and glided smoothly away.

"I think magnets are the key to understanding gravity," I explained. "Magnetism is just a *subset* of gravity. Magnetically charged particles are singing a little love song—just like gravity, only maybe in a slightly different language and much, much louder." I paused, trying to come up with an example.

"Think about Chambodia," I said, referring to the local nickname for the city of Chamblee on the north side of Atlanta, just south of Doraville. "Lots of Cambodians love America, and move here to live and work. But it's only natural to want to live around others who speak the same language and share cultural traits. So you get big clusters of Cambodians living together in communities. Atlanta is like gravity: just a big ol' melting pot of free love for all. Chamblee

122

is a subset of Atlanta, but stands out because it acts like a magnet. Cambodians are attracted to Atlanta, but are even more attracted by a love for one another.

"It's harder to see levity because we're so attuned to the more obvious gravity. But I think levity is hiding in plain view. Why does the earth spin on its axis? Angular momentum? Centrifugal force? Absence of resisting force? I think it's much simpler than all of that—though those things obviously play a part. I think the main driver is an expression of the opposing forces of gravity and levity, resisting each other in a circular direction. This causes levity to get bound up in a vortex at the center of the earth—a place we don't visit, so we can't see it.

"Look, everything has to obey the same laws in order for our reality to be what it is. Think about the Earth and other planets relentlessly trekking around the sun for millions of years. Now think about atoms with orbiting particles, pretty much doing the same thing. Just about every science book for kids compares atoms to solar systems. But is it just some weird coincidence that atoms and solar systems seem to behave so similarly, even to the point of spinning particles? What if atoms really are little solar systems with planets just like ours, only in an unimaginably tiny dimension? Maybe one of the electrons is a planet just like Earth. What if the Earth is just a tiny particle circulating around a tiny atom in some super gigantic dude's fingernail?"

"Whoa, that's some seriously messed-up shit. bro," Jorge inserted from behind me. I hadn't noticed his return.

I shook my head and continued: "Our world, our reality, all matter, everything... it all has to obey the same simple set of physical laws. Everything strives to achieve the same state of being.

"Whatever it is—gravity, magnetism, attraction, whatever you want to call it—it has to be extremely simple. So simple that even a single-celled amoeba can use it effectively to attract and glue together enough atoms to replicate itself. Even more basic than chemistry is attraction. At its most basic, it's just ones and zeros. On, off. Positive, negative. And it requires no energy: it just *is*.

"I think maybe magnetism is just an exaggerated form of gravity. And maybe magnetic waves are just a byproduct of the way certain atoms interact—like heat being a byproduct of a chemical reaction.

"The key to understanding gravity, then—the thing that ties everything together—is understanding magnets. For every action there is an equal and opposite reaction. Gravity has an opposite; it simply *has* to. And that opposite is just as important as the reflection. Magnets sing the same love song, only louder and at a slightly different pitch. Which is good, because we maybe have a better chance of hearing it."

"Atomic love, fine, whatever, I get it," said Flip impatiently. "But I still don't understand how the board levitates."

"I think I accidentally tapped into the channel that Atomic Love broadcasts on," I said. "This device sends a tiny positive electrical signal through a wire, to a lead attached to the aluminum. Along the way something happens to the frequency as it travels over a magnet. And all the bonded aluminum atoms start singing the atomic love song in reverse, causing it to repel. The force is strong enough to lift Jorge off the ground. If I switched it to the negative lead, the board would stick to the floor with so much force that Jorge wouldn't be able to pick it up. And at the same time, it acts like an unspecific magnet, focusing on whatever is closest to it, like a glass table or hardwood floors or whatever."

"So, okay, that sounds like a good thing. Why would anybody want to kill you over that?" asked Flip.

"Energy," Jessica answered for me, opening the black box on the board that had been returned to the table. She pulled out the nine-volt battery attached to two wires. "This is all the power that's needed to lift a two hundred and fifty pound man." She glanced at Jorge. Her guess was easily a hundred pounds short, so no offense was taken.

"So? That still seems like a good thing. I don't get the problem here."

I took the reins again. "The amount of work done far exceeds the amount of energy put in. So say goodbye to fossil fuel. Say goodbye to nuclear power plants. And say hello to an infinite supply of ultra-cheap energy."

Flip thought about that for a long moment. Finally, in a very low, very serious tone, he said, "Oh shit. We're fucked."

The words were heavy. Even Clyde had to be rethinking things. As for me, all I wanted to do was crawl my aching body into bed and sleep forever. Maybe I'd wake up as an Eskimo who'd been having a nightmare about being an Emory student. Maybe I'd go ice fishing tomorrow.

"We're fucked," Flip repeated quietly.

Clyde grinned. "No we're not."

Chapter 12
OPERATION ZG

"**T**his better be important," growled Jim Giles groggily, blinking into the glaring light, trying to identify who had dared to flip the switch.

"There's been a development, sir," a woman's voice replied. The door closed hastily.

Atlanta. I'm in Atlanta. Operation ZG. A development?

Giles kicked his feet of the couch, sat up, fastened his top button, and adjusted his tie, all in one fluid motion. But he felt his age more than a little as he struggled off the couch. At fifty-two, Giles had finally discovered that there was a limit to how many nights he could string together with little sleep.

As bright as the light had been in the tiny, windowless office, his destination was much brighter. And unpleasantly noisy.

The Order had taken possession of a hangar at Peachtree-DeKalb Airport, a small commuter hub in Chamblee on the northeast side of Atlanta. Giles glanced at his watch: four a.m. He had only been asleep for a little over an hour. And during that time, the number of personnel had multiplied. There were now eighty-plus computer stations and at least a hundred agents. It looked like ground control for a shuttle launch.

At the center of it all, they were ready to go.

As Giles approached, a young man brought him up to speed. "Sir, police found the car outside Chattanooga. It was on fire when they arrived." The agent pointed up at a big screen that showed a live feed in infrared: firefighters dousing the fire.

"What do we know?" Giles asked, looking to Agent Redding, a more familiar face.

"The car was abandoned before it was set ablaze," Redding answered. "No bodies, sir. The license plate was wrong, but FBI chatter indicates the VIN number belongs to Jessica Osgood's vehicle."

Thomas Redding was a very large, square-jawed beast of a man. Everything about him, including the short-cropped mane standing at attention on top his head, bespoke ruthless military purpose. He had been recruited directly out the U.S. Armed Forces Delta program. Earlier that day, Redding had led a mission that, in a first for his career, had failed. It had been an attempt to scoop up two subjects, a couple of college kids.

The fact that this college kid, Dale Adams, had been able to evade a six-man team of elite operatives was nothing short of astounding. Yes, there had been interference from outside sources, and yes, the kid had caught a female operative off guard. And in a stroke of bad luck, air support had arrived about thirty seconds too late. Still, Adams had managed to escape a hardened team of pros. Less amazing, but still impressive, was the fact that he had managed to disappear right from under police and FBI noses, seeming to vanish into thin air.

Adams had earned a modicum of begrudging respect from Giles.

"What are the witnesses saying? Do we know which direction they're heading?" asked Giles, studying the monitor.

"And where is this feed coming from?"

"No witnesses. Chattanooga is a few miles west of the location. FBI think's it's the probable destination. And the feed is from a drone, sir."

"A drone? The NSA is providing us a feed? Why the hell are *they* here?" demanded Giles.

"That's an interesting question, Jim." came the answer from behind Giles.

Giles turned and found himself shocked to be facing Nathan Letson. Here in the middle of an operation. A Council member.

This was very much against protocol. During eighteen years with the Order, Giles had been involved in countless operations. And at least once every other year, some event had managed to spark a critical undertaking like this. Yet in all his years, no member of Parliament had *ever* put a boot on the ground. What's more, Giles was fairly certain there was no such precedent in the Order's four hundred and thirty-five year history.

"It's good to see you, sir," Giles said cautiously. Was his leadership on this operation being questioned?

"Likewise," replied Letson. Nathan Letson was a portly man with frazzled white hair. His clothes were well worn, probably purchased in the eighties, and likely slept in for the last few days. For this man, consideration of appearance was a wasteful mental enterprise.

Despite attire and hygiene that could easily get him mistaken for a guy who sleeps in his car, Nathan Letson was the most powerful man on the planet.

But what was he doing here? Letson didn't have the military or intelligence background that would be necessary to run an operation like this. Letson had been a philosopher of some note, recruited by the Order after a series of papers he'd written in the sixties about the relationship between

128

economic conditions and fertility rates. Assuming personal command of an operation like this didn't make sense.

"You needn't be concerned about our presence here. We have perfect faith in your skills and abilities. You have been tasked, we approve of your approach in this matter, and we want you to see it through. I'm here only as an observer—and to deliver a message." Letson spoke kindly, as if soothing a child.

Turning and placing his hand on the shoulder of a tall, lanky man in a tweed jacket, Letson continued. "This is Dr. Jacob Stevenson, professor emeritus at Caltech, still active with certain endeavors at JPL. He can answer your question about the NSA presence."

Stevenson wasn't quite ready for his cue; he was too busy absorbing the antlike action taking place throughout the hangar. He cleared his throat. "Right. Yes. The National Security Agency got involved because of an anomaly reported by JSpOC. The report got sent up the chain at U.S. STRATCOM and was eventually handed over to the NSA for follow-up."

Letson recognized confusion on Giles's face. "U.S. Strategic Command has a space control mission run by the Joint Functional Component Command for Space. JSpOC is the Joint Space Operations Center, a division of JFCC-Space. Alphabet soup, I know," Letson said. "Basically JSpOC is a bunch of space garbage men."

"I'm not sure I'd put it that way," replied Stevenson. The conversation had his full attention now. "JSpOC's mission is to detect, track, and identify all man-made objects in Earth orbit. Because the Earth is constantly bombarded by meteors, certain algorithms are in place to screen out that activity as white noise. Ten days ago these algorithms kicked out a series of errors. Or at least what techs initially thought were errors." Stevenson leaned in toward Giles to convey the excitement.

"What they had actually detected were objects coming from Earth and burning up as they left the atmosphere!"

Giles shrugged. "And the NSA tracked it to our target? Do they believe it's a weapon?"

Stevenson was flabbergasted at the obtuse nature of this response. "You don't get it. The objects burned up in the atmosphere!"

"Yes, *sir*. I heard you, *sir*," Giles returned sharply. "That's why you guys protect space shuttles with heat tiles, so they don't burn up, right? Does the NSA think this kid is building missiles?"

"Wrong! We protect shuttles for reentry!" Dr. Stevenson was animated now. "Outside of magnetic rail guns in a laboratory or ballistics requiring cutting-edge chemical propulsion under very controlled circumstances, there simply is no practical way to achieve the kind of velocities necessary to create enough friction to burn objects up while *leaving* the atmosphere! Certainly not at a nearly perfectly vertical trajectory! Yet JSpOC recorded *six* such events in the space of *three minutes*. This is the most amazing—"

Letson interrupted, pulling the professor back by his shoulder. Stevenson was so excited that he was practically shouting in Giles's face.

"Jim, I brought Dr. Stevenson in here because I wanted him to impress upon you the significance of what we're all taking part in here. Forgive his exuberance. You will understand in a moment. What's important is that you realize that this is the single most important mission you have ever run for us." As Letson released the doctor's shoulder, he clarified. "In fact, obtaining this technology is the most important mission the *Order* has ever had."

Stevenson had been released, but now his lips moved as he struggled for the right words. Finally his shoulders relaxed and he gestured at a cluster of big screens. They were displaying an endless muted cycle of the videos that had been posted to YouTube under the username ZG_Enterprise, an account owned by Dale Adams.

"Each one of these videos appears to be demonstrating a different phenomenon caused by manipulating a never-before-observed principle of physics. Your techs have analyzed the raw video exactly as it was uploaded—taken directly from YouTube's servers—and have yet to find any sign of tampering or editing. Further," he paused, pointing at the screen in the middle, which showed Dale Adams wearing large black earmuffs and laughing as he launched paint cans into oblivion, "the time stamp embedded in this particular video correlates closely to the timing of the anomalies recorded by JSpOC. Additionally, the NSA has followed the trajectory of the objects back to Dale Adams's place of employment. It appears to be a near-certainty that this is not just an elaborate hoax, which was our initial take, as you might imagine.

"Despite this evidence, I still would like to perform my own tests before jumping to any speculative conclusions. However, when Nathan came to me, he asked me to set aside any doubts, and just assume the videos are real. What he wanted to know was very simple: If gravity could truly be controlled as demonstrated in the videos, what were the implications?"

Stevenson paused, wrestling with too many thoughts.

"The most obvious benefit is an infinite source of force—a means of powering devices that create usable forms of energy," he said, pointing to a screen that showed the guts of a shake light that had been pulled apart so the camera could witness a magnet traveling up and down through a coil to generate power. Eventually a little puff of dark smoke appeared, as a capacitor, overwhelmed by repeated energy surges, melted down. "This is a very crude device, but it does demonstrate that by controlling the force of gravity to drive a simple Faraday generator, energy can actually be *created*.

"Now, I know what you're all thinking," Stevenson added quickly, casting about to see who was preparing to laugh at him. "Energy can n ither be created nor destroyed, right? But if gravity can be controlled, it seems clear that there exist possibilities outside of Newton's Law of Conservation of Energy. This young man appears to be demonstrating a clear exception," Stevenson said, pointing to a screen that showed Dale Adams gliding around a parking lot on his hoverboard. "Assuming something as impossible as a perfect transfer of stored electricity into a simple motor that could do the work of lifting, like a lawnmower engine, we've calculated that a fully charged nine-volt battery should only be able to lift a one-hundred-eighty-pound mass, such as a man standing on a hoverboard, for eight point four seconds!

"Of course, e equals mc squared, so, theoretically, the work of lifting could be extended indefinitely if we allowed for the mass of the chemicals inside the battery to be consumed," Stevenson said, glancing around to see who was going down that path. "But the odds of a single person unlocking cold fusion and gravity at the same moment are laughable. It simply cannot be. No, it appears as though the battery isn't being used to do the actual work of lifting; it's merely sending a signal to tell a force of antigravity to repel the board away from the ground."

"Sir," said a quiet female voice behind Giles. She was tapping his shoulder.

"Not now," Giles dismissed her gruffly.

"The implication is this," continued Stevenson. "That the forces of attraction and repulsion are not necessarily tied to a constant, in the unchangeable sense of the word. According to the law of universal gravitation, the attractive force between two bodies is proportional to the product of their masses, and inversely proportional to the square of the distance between them. The constant of proportionality, the big G, is the gravitational constant. But these videos seem to suggest that the big G can be unchained from the two masses and, instead of behaving as a constant, act more like a magnetic vector that relies on an input that can be *tuned*. It seems to suggest that the mass of the two objects can be made less relevant than the variant of a bond between them, something that can actually be controlled. This has *fascinating* implications to the mathematics of field theory because—"

"Sir," interrupted Giles. "Sir, I'm sorry, but you're losing me here."

"He's right, Jacob," Letson added. "Please, time is of the essence."

"Yes, yes, I'm sorry. I digress," agreed Stevenson. "What's important is that the amount of attraction—or repulsion—that two objects have for one another appears to be something that is communicated, whether that be through electromagnetic current, or gravitational waves, or something else entirely. But the important thing is that information passes between two objects, simulating an awareness of each other's existence, relative size, and distance. Controlling this communication—and the attractive or repulsive force that it generates—has tremendous potential for uses that can be translated into limitless energy sources."

Stevenson looked to Letson for approval that he was back on track. "Currently, about six point four percent of all electricity consumed in the United States every day is generated as a byproduct of gravity. Because of gravity, water flows downhill. The Hoover Dam is able to generate electricity by directing water flow through chambers where the mechanical energy of flowing water spins turbines. The turbines turn a shaft that drives a Faraday electric generator, converting the mechanical energy to electrical energy."

Stevenson knew everyone was waiting for the payoff. He chose his next words carefully. "If you could point gravity away from a fixed source on one side of a turbine, you could cause a turbine to spin. As the antigravity force pushed one propeller down and away, another propeller would enter the field and be pushed down and away, and so on. Potentially, this turbine could spin indefinitely, so long as the signal that inspires antigravity continued. The result, it seems, would be an extraction of energy."

"Sir," the young agent spoke cautiously into Giles's ear. Again she was brushed off.

Now Stevenson's excitement was growing again. "The ability to direct gravitational force and the relative strength of that force opens the door to ways of creating mechanical energy from dimensions unknown to physics! It's possible that a Faraday generator isn't the most efficient way to generate electricity, but even if we were to limit ourselves to Faraday's principles, these generators could easily be scaled to fit the application. Large power plants could feed even bigger electrical grids for cities. Or, even more interesting, scaled way down to, say, power a household... or even an individual appliance, like a stove or a television."

"Please, Jacob, please get to the reason why I brought you here," admonished Letson.

Stevenson bit his lower lip with frustration. "Fine," he said reluctantly. "Potential for energy aside, there's something far more exciting to consider, something that will alter humanity forever. This kid has unlocked—"

"Sir! I really must insist, sir!"

"Speak," commanded Giles with exasperation, holding a finger up to indicate that Stevenson should give him a moment.

"A new video has been uploaded," blurted the nervous

young lady.

Giles turned, giving his full attention to the operative. "Well, put it on the screen already!"

The monitor showed what appeared to be a still shot of hardwood flooring. "Turn on the audio."

"It *is* on, sir."

"Dear murderous fuckers," a voice said. Giles recognized it as the voice of Dale Adams. "Did it ever occur to you that you could simply *buy* my silence? You have until two p.m. to place fifty million dollars into my account at First National or I will publish step-by-step directions on how to build my device. After you clear our names of all criminal allegations, I will hand over the device and you can do as you please with it. The end, fuckers."

The hardwood faded to black and YouTube offered a number of other videos to choose from. The view switched out of full screen to show the YouTube page. Somebody highlighted a selection of text.

It was a response below the video, posted by the YouTube user InterestedParty_ATL: "Acknowledged."

"When was this uploaded?"

"Twenty minutes ago, sir. Time stamp says it was actually recorded about ten minutes before that."

"Can we track the IP?"

"Well, about that, sir." Now she was even more nervous; her blouse revealed sweat stains under her arms. "We may have made a bit of a mistake. Mr. Adams's profile made no mention of skills as a hacker…"

"Just spit it out already!"

"The person who posted the video made no effort to cover the IP, which was expected. It led directly to a computer, one that was not behind a firewall. We thought we had him. So we decided to do a bit of reconnaissance, find out who the computer belonged to, see what information we could obtain from the hard drive." Her throat bobbed nervously. "It was a honeypot, sir. Just a trap. It shut down moments after we got in."

"So where is he?"

"Well, we don't know, sir. The computer was just a random server, one of thousands sitting in rack space in a datacenter near Hartsfield Airport. Because the power supply was cut, we have no way to pick up the IP that was controlling it, sir."

Giles was processing. Adams was *not* a hacker, nor was Jessica Osgood.

"Dismissed," Giles told the young agent.

But she stood her ground nervously, unable to obey. "Sir, there is… there is just one more thing. Sir, we've been compromised. Within moments of realizing we had made a mistake, we were subjected to a massive denial-of-service attack. It only took a few minutes to overcome, but when we did, we discovered that a text file had been placed on our system."

She held up a printout and read: "Last warning. We have provided you with a sound business solution to your problem. Further acts of hostility will result in an automated program that will distribute to various news agencies a do-it-yourself plan for building the device that you wish to destroy, as well as a detailed summary of recent events. Comply with our request immediately. Cease and desist your destructive efforts; clear our names; and pay us for our silence. Or else."

She finished reading and looked around at the stunned faces, then added: "We believe this threat is real, sir. We followed protocol and covered our tracks. Despite that, tracking us back isn't terribly impressive, though it was amazingly fast. And a DOS is easy enough once you have a target. But compromising *our* firewall to leave a file directly on our server?" She shook her head with disbelief. "Whoever did this is a very gifted hacker, sir. World class. Instead of us finding *him*, he found *us*. I'm not sure if it matters, but you should know that he now knows exactly where we are, sir."

A slow smile crept over Giles's face. The woman had never seen him smile, and wasn't sure she liked it. But she had been expecting fire and brimstone, so a crooked smile felt like a win. With nothing more to add, she escaped the spotlight as quickly as possible.

Giles turned to Letson, still smiling.

"Instead of terminating the Greener team, I think we should let this thing play out," Giles said, pointing at the word "Acknowledged." "He's a slippery little devil. This exchange might be our best shot at flushing him out."

Letson studied Giles for a long moment, then smiled warmly. "I'm glad you like him as much as I do. But don't get too attached."

Stevenson fidgeted impatiently, clearly annoyed with the interruption, and now greatly alarmed that this young man might intentionally be left in a dangerous situation.

"Maybe it hasn't *all* been chance and dumb luck," Letson continued grimly, ignoring Stevenson. "But don't forget he's just a kid with no agency training. Letting this 'play out' sounds logical, but if we don't step on Greener, there's always the chance they'll achieve their intent. And we need this kid alive. We certainly don't want some automated program spreading do-it-yourself directions out there. If we let this continue, then we must have our thumb on every player, at all times." Turning to the doctor, he said, "Jacob, would you please—"

"You don't understand! Humanity has an expiration date!" Stevenson practically shouted, not waiting for Letson to finish. "We don't know when, we don't know how, but eventually an extinction event *must* occur. These people you say are trying to kill him—you have to stop them! This child is carrying the key to extending the survival of our species, indefinitely."

"Please," said Letson, putting a calming hand on Stevenson's shoulder. "Just explain why."

Chapter 13
THE JESUS CHANNEL

"Shiiiiiit," Clyde said, drawing the word out slowly. "I look like a little kid in his daddy's clothes."

Flip laughed. Clyde was right: the suit was way too big.

"Dude, don't sweat it. He's gonna be stirred up, he won't have time to notice what you're wearing. He'll glance at you, see the tie, and think nothing more—except that he's pissed off."

Jorge yawned. "Can't we take a nap first?"

"Y'all need to look alive," snapped Flip, digging in his pocket. "You got one hour to get there—you better be fucking wide awake."

Flip dropped a tiny, clear Ziploc bag on the desk in front of Clyde. Clyde shook his head at the contents.

"Not my thing," he said, pushing the baggy toward Jorge.

Jorge dug in his pocket for his keys. "Yeah, I could use a bump."

"You'll have about a half-hour window," Flip said. "Kelner's bringing a couple of his OGS boys. They'll handle any heavy lifting."

"Those puto-ass skins better not fuck this shit up," muttered Jorge.

Kelner might have been a racist psychopath, but he'd be a handy guy to have around if the shit hit the fan. Of that, Flip was certain.

"You do your job and they'll do theirs," Flip said, and handed a piece of paper to Clyde.

"You didn't have to print directions, I've got my phone," Clyde said.

"You can't use your phone," Flip replied. "Turn them off right now, so you don't forget. Don't leave any trails—especially digital."

Flip doubted his friends had the remotest clue how scary that warning really was. Within ten minutes of posting Dale's video to YouTube, Flip's IP had been tracked back. The only way anyone could accomplish that would be if they had direct access to Google's servers. Only God himself could pull that off—or somebody with the juice of Edward Snowden's NSA.

"Kelner should be there when you get there, but if you need to call him, the number's right here," Flip said, pointing to the sheet in Clyde's hand. "Use the burner and get rid of it before you get back here."

Clyde turned and punched Jorge's shoulder, spilling powder on his lap. "One's enough, man. I need you awake, not wired."

Clyde wasn't looking forward to a long ride with Jorge talking a mile a minute. Jorge said nothing. He just returned the baggy to the desk and sullenly stuck his keys in his pocket.

"You can take the Benz," Flip said, offering his keys to Clyde. "Just make sure to switch the plates before you get there. I don't want some old man writing down my number."

"You sure? I can take the van. You know we're—"

"Yeah, I know," Flip said, cutting Clyde off. "But the van would stick out like a sore thumb. Take the Benz, man. If it gets fucked up, I'll just buy another. You don't have time to boost something that fits the neighborhood."

Clyde looked off into the darkness of Flip's "Crib". He could see the shadow of Dale sleeping on the couch. Clyde had been down a lot of shady roads, but this one made him very nervous. He was tempted to wake Dale up.

"You're sure he'll be there?" Clyde asked.

Flip shrugged. "No. But that's his schedule right there." He pointed at the screen, knowing his friend could never appreciate the skill that it represented. "He has to be downtown in two hours. We know where he lives, and we know where he has to be. We're sure he has to pass this spot at some point. You guys just might have to wait a while."

"All right," Clyde returned, unhappy but resigned. Turning to Jorge: "Let's roll, Kemo."

* * *

Riverside Drive. Atlanta's hidden enclave for the wealthy—Rodeo Drive with a southern accent—is tucked just inside the perimeter on the north side of town. Riverside is a tiny, low-volume exit off 285, nestled between super-busy thoroughfares. The kind of exit more appropriate for a lazy country road in the middle of nowhere. It simply has no business connecting to a twelve-lane highway.

A narrow bridge crosses the freeway, feeding a two-lane road that winds through the densely wooded hills. Long driveways connect and meander off behind the trees, where the moneyed rest their heads. Roswell and Marietta are for athletes, rappers, and dot-commers. Riverside and Buckhead are home to the ruling class.

The sun would be up soon. Passing the occasional car, Clyde was thankful for the Mercedes as camouflage. Even if he'd had time to gank a ride, he probably wouldn't have been able to come up with something this good.

It only took a few moments to find the target intersection,

a four-way stop in a quiet neighborhood. Two blocks beyond the stop sign, Clyde found a side street. Turning around in a driveway, he parked a block up, killed the lights, and waited.

The bar phone started buzzing on the dashboard. It was a cheap Nokia burner. Clyde snatched it and hit the green button. "Yeah?"

"Just saw y'all go by, calling to let you know we're here," said a voice with a thick southern drawl. Kelner.

"All right," Clyde replied and then hung up.

Thankfully Jorge was quiet. He wasn't sleeping, he was just sitting there quietly in the dim glow from the console. Jorge might talk a big game, but he was solid when it mattered.

"I've got a bad feeling about this," Jorge said quietly.

Me too, Clyde thought.

Shit. Jesus was issuing warnings to both of them. If circumstances were different, Clyde would have bailed on this enterprise in a heartbeat. Never doubt the Finger of God when it pokes you.

Clyde had always been particular about that, even as a kid. His father was a preacher, so to him, good-old-fashioned superstition got translated into God's influence. Clyde was convinced that God would give you hints, and that you sure as hell better pay attention when he did. What some would see as intuition that may or may not mean anything, Clyde saw as God's advice, demanding some sort of action. And God offered Clyde a lot of advice, even in some particularly ungodly types of circumstances.

Take creeping, for instance.

Creeping, for the uninitiated, is the practice of "borrowing" the contents of a vehicle without first gaining formal permission from the vehicle's owner. Work was scarce for fifteen- and sixteen-year-old kids growing up in Doraville. Selling drugs was easy enough, but it came with its own set of hazards, unless you were running for somebody else.

Creeping, on the other hand, was easy money.

Their typical method of operation was to find a street they intended to victimize. The driver would kill the headlights and idle slowly down the street while two or three kids ran along on either side, hitting cars. They kept close to their own car, so if anybody saw or heard anything out of place he would just whistle, and everyone would pile in and scram. But Clyde insisted on keeping God's channel open, even while creeping. That meant that if someone simply had a bad vibe, they were supposed to whistle.

Dale had hated that rule, because it got used so much— usually by Jorge. Dale had always felt like he was missing out on all the good stuff because people were just punking out and blaming it on God.

"So what?" Clyde had asked rhetorically. "Even if he's right only one out of ten times, it's still not worth the risk. You gotta listen to your heart. Jesus lives there."

One night in particular, Dale had found the ultimate cherry: a '71 Oldsmobile Cutlass lowrider with shiny rims and tinted windows. A gangsta-mobile that was sure to be loaded for boom. On the dash, through the tint, the signature red blinking of a Cobra II alarm, a simple system that was attached to the stereo and would use the speakers to make a stink if the doors or trunk were opened without a key. It lacked window sensors.

If you do it right, breaking a car window makes almost no noise. Dale took the edge of his screwdriver and, pressing it flat against the front corner of the driver's window, wedged it as far as he could down the crack between the glass and the door. Taking a deep breath, he pulled the handle slowly but steadily toward himself. The pressure built and suddenly gave. With a muffled pop, the window spidered completely, but didn't shatter. He withdrew the screwdriver and gently pushed the window, crumbling it quietly into the vehicle.

Just as he began to admire the Sony heaven within, God told Jorge to whistle.

Dale looked around quickly for a threat. The night was black, crickets were singing, and the only light was from a streetlamp way down the block. He shook his head with frustration as he watched two shadowy figures hurriedly climb into their car. Dale's mouth was watering for the box that was surely in the trunk. No way was he passing on eight hundred bucks for three minutes of work. God could wait.

Dale climbed through the window and began to dismantle the sound system. He was pulling the head unit from its mounting when Clyde hissed, "Come on, man. Let's get the fuck out of here."

They had reversed back and were now beside Dale. He ignored them. Clyde got louder and louder, ever more insistent.

Then Dale heard little Mikey say: "Oh. Shit."

That caught Dale's attention. He looked up to see a set of headlights just on the other side of the streetlamp. The car was sitting still, bright lights pointed in their direction. When a spotlight turned on, Dale's heart froze. Mikey's first instinct was to hit the gas. They went screeching away from Dale, still in reverse. Mikey missed a turn, jumped the curb, and tore up the front lawn of somebody's house. They had left Dale behind.

Dale looked back up the street. The police cruiser now had its flashing lights on—and was flying down the street, right at him. But it never even slowed as it went by. Mikey managed to put his car in gear and came charging back—straight at the cop.

The officer swerved off the road to turn around as Mikey flew by. It appeared that Mikey had a good lead and maybe a chance, but he had forgotten to turn on his headlights.

Dale had watched as the fleeing car became a shadow in

the distance, then briefly appeared in living color as it passed beneath a streetlamp, then disappeared completely into the blackness beyond.

A split second later, *Kaboom*.

Without benefit of headlights, Mikey had failed to see the parked car just on the other side of the streetlamp.

The explosion shattered the quiet night. A shower of sparks lit up that end of the street. A few moments passed. Dale eased himself down even lower in the car. The cruiser coasted by slowly—inexplicably slowly, until Dale heard the officer's panicked voice pleading for backup. Dale thought the cop was going to stop right next to him, but he didn't. The officer's siren was off, but the sudden silence of night creatures was louder than any siren.

When the cop was a safe distance away, Dale climbed out of the car and slipped between two houses, into the woods beyond, even as bedroom windows began to dot the street with light.

Were it not for the dumb luck of Mikey's stupidity scaring the snot out of that cop, they would never have had time to escape the stolen car and disappear into the woods. Jorge had been in the back and was fine, but Mikey's arm was broken in two places and Clyde's eyebrow was pasted to the windshield. Still, they'd had time to extract themselves from the crushed vehicle. Clyde was thereafter convinced that God was trying to tell him something. He got out of the creeping business for good.

"Heads up," Jorge said quietly, interrupting Clyde's thoughts.

Clyde had seen it too. He eased down the street, turned left, and accelerated to catch up with the dark sedan. It was the right vehicle, a black BMW 5-series with a plate that started with JKL. It was just before six a.m., and there was nobody else on the road.

As the BMW's brake lights lit up, Clyde warned: "Watch out for airbags."

Crunch. Clyde rammed solidly into the rear of the Beamer, but at under ten miles per hour. No airbags. Sounds of broken plastic pulling apart could be heard as Clyde reversed back a few feet.

Clyde poured some soda in his lap, then stepped out, tucking a nine in his back waistband. *Shit*—he spotted a pair of joggers. But they were headed away, and appeared not to have noticed the "accident."

The driver's tinted window slid down as Clyde approached. A young guy?

"Everybody all right?" Clyde asked. Glancing in the back, he was relieved to see the target.

So the young guy was a driver. More likely a bodyguard. Shit.

The driver studied Clyde coolly.

"I am *so* sorry, I was checking email on the way to the office," Clyde explained. He shook his head irritably, looking down at his pants. "I spilled coffee everywhere!"

The man continued to watch Clyde silently. Finally: "Yeah, we're all right."

"Oh, good," Clyde said, breathing a sigh of relief. Pointing behind the vehicle at Jorge, Clyde added: "Don't worry, it's not real bad. My car's worse than yours. I broke your taillight, though. My buddy's calling the police."

The man in the back said something that Clyde couldn't hear. The driver was studying the rearview mirror out of the corner of his eye. Yeah, definitely a bodyguard. This guy was on his toes.

The driver seemed to relax, seeing Jorge holding a phone to his ear. "Tell your friend he can hang up; we don't have the time for police," he said. "We can just exchange insurance."

"Sure, sure. That's much better, thanks," Clyde said,

feigning relief. Turning to Jorge: "Never mind, Jim. You can hang up. We're just going to swap insurance cards."

"Can you step back, please?" the driver asked.

"Huh? Sure," Clyde answered, stepping away from the door and toward the front of the vehicle, pretending not to be aware of the bodyguard's motive for backing him away. The bodyguard climbed out slowly, clearly displeased that he had to split his attention between both right and left. He kept his focus on Clyde, who was closer.

"Hi, I'm Jim," Jorge said, approaching quickly, hand extended.

One square look at Jorge and the man knew he was in trouble. He went for his shoulder holster.

"Nope," Clyde said quietly, pressing a barrel to the bodyguard's neck. "Easy, buddy. Nobody needs to get hurt."

Jorge reached into the man's suit jacket and extracted a pistol, then quickly patted him down, finding a snub-nosed .38 on his ankle.

Headlights approached from behind.

"Just keep cool," Clyde told the man, tucking his pistol hand in a pocket. "I got no problem shooting you or anybody else if I have to."

An Audi S7. It eased up beside the "accident," its passenger window sliding open. "Talk about a lousy way to start the day! Everybody okay? Need me to call for help?"

"No, we're good," Clyde replied, smiling calmly. "Thanks, though."

The bodyguard said nothing.

"All right... well, good luck, then."

The window began sliding back up and the Audi eased away. Suddenly the back passenger door of the BMW flew open and an older man, wearing a suit, went barreling off into the shadows.

"Fuck. I got it," Jorge said, shaking his head.

"No. You just get this fucker in the trunk," Clyde replied through gritted teeth, smiling and waiting for the Audi to leave. Had the driver noticed?

The Audi's light was blinking for a left turn. After a safe wait, it turned left and pulled off. It was in no rush. Clyde breathed a sigh of relief.

"You got him?"

"Open the fucking trunk," Jorge told the bodyguard, ignoring Clyde's question.

Clyde rounded the BMW and ran off into darkness in the direction the passenger had gone. The guy was fat and old, probably in his late sixties. No way he was getting far. Plus, his escape route was poorly chosen. He had run into the woods for cover, instead of running down the street toward the nearest house.

Clyde ran for a minute, then stopped. It was pitch black. The underbrush was thick, and he had already caught a branch in the face twice.

He stood in the silent darkness and listened. *Fuck.* This guy was probably hiding. Clyde didn't have a flashlight, so no way he was going to find him.

Crack. A branch snapping underfoot, about twenty yards to the right.

It took only a moment for Clyde to find the man lying on the ground under some bushes, panting and hiding his eyes like a little kid hoping that "if I can't see him, he can't see me."

"Mr. Simons, I need you to get up."

"You—you're just going to kill me," Simons sputtered. "They got everyone else already. I know I'm the last loose end."

"No. I'm not going to kill you. Just get up, we—"

"I've got money!" Simons cried out. "Lots of it—cash. Five hundred thousand, just sitting in a safe at my house!

148

That has to be way more than what Greener is paying."

Clyde considered that. "I'm not with 'Greener.'"

Simons looked up, confused. "But…"

"Get up. Right now—get the fuck up."

"Oh? Oh. I see. You're with *them*?"

A flicker of hope danced in Simons's eye. He climbed to his feet and dusted his suit off.

"Move," Clyde demanded, pointing his gun toward the street. *Them?*

Back at the street, the trunk of the Mercedes was open, and Jorge was sitting in the driver's seat of the BMW.

Clyde looked up and down the road for a long moment, then shoved Simons toward the Benz. "You're getting in the trunk."

"Oh come on, please?"

Clyde said nothing—he just pushed the older man toward the car. Into the trunk he went.

Traffic was picking up. Two cars stopped to the right. The driver in the second car lowered her window, but Clyde waved her off. "We're all right, thanks!"

Turning his attention to the trunk: "Hands."

"That's not necessary," Simons protested, even as he offered his hands.

"No. Behind your back."

Simons struggled to comply. Clyde cinched his wrists together with a thick zip tie.

With Simons and the bodyguard both stowed away in the cars' trunks, Jorge led the way in the BMW, and Clyde followed in Flip's car. They got back onto the interstate and went three exits up. Jorge got off, jogged down a block, and parked in front of an abandoned Mexican restaurant, as planned. The bodyguard was kicking the inner wall of the trunk. Jorge banged the trunk and the man stopped.

Clyde waited, wondering where Kelner was, while Jorge

switched the plates on the Benz. The bar phone buzzed as Jorge climbed in the passenger seat beside Clyde.

"Yeah," Clyde answered.

"Y'all got company," Kelner said. "Blue Chrysler at the Stop-N-Go."

Clyde glanced toward the gas station across the street, trying to seem casual. "Got 'em."

"Take your time when you get on the highway. Soon as we make our move, make tracks."

"Okay," Clyde replied, tossing the phone onto the dash.

"'S'up?" Jorge asked as Clyde eased onto the road.

"We're being followed. Kelner's gonna take 'em out on the highway."

"Shit," Jorge said, yanking the seatbelt across. "I told you man, I had a bad feeling. First a fucking bodyguard, then the dude runs, now this." Jorge was silent for a moment, looking over his shoulder. "What are they gonna do? Crazy-ass redneck putos—they better *not* shoot nobody."

Clyde didn't answer. Both of them had been touched. He should have just aborted this whole thing before it started.

It was a quarter after six. Morning rush was just starting. Traffic was heavy, but mostly flowing. Lots of brake lights in the two right lanes, though. Clyde merged over four lanes; the Chrysler followed suit.

Where was Kelner? *There.* A white pickup, one lane over, just behind and to the right of the Chrysler.

Suddenly the front of the pickup veered hard into the rear of the Chrysler. Headlights, taillights, headlights, *boom.* The Chrysler spun out of control, skidded out of its lane, and plowed into the cab of an eighteen-wheeler. The rear of the big truck jackknifed, swinging out and catching up with the front.

Clyde gunned it, darting two lanes left even as chaos exploded behind him, cars veering wildly this way and that to avoid the carnage. Weaving smoothly from lane to lane, Clyde quickly put some distance behind him. No Chrysler in sight.

"Gooooood morning, Atlanta," quipped Jorge in a white-guy radio voice. "You can stick a fork in the north side already, pileup on 285. But what else is new, kiddos?"

Chapter 14
STRAIGHT TO HELL

"**W**akey wakey, Booksy wooksy!"

The words were hushed, but loud enough to be heard. Unfortunately, my mind was too befuddled to comprehend. My eyes flashed open in time to see the shadow of a giant ass descending upon my face.

Fuck!

The side of my face was buried deep in the couch cushion, pinned beneath the unspeakable. I cursed up a muffled blue streak as I struggled to free myself. The only thing that prevented me from killing him was the fact that Jorge kept whispering for me to be quiet. This forced me to think about *why*, which calmed me just enough for rational thought.

Finally free, I cast about to get my bearings. The only light in the room was from the soft glow of electronic devices. A couch. A coffee table. A television. A big room. I'd fallen asleep in Flip's warehouse. Jorge didn't want me to wake Jessica, who must have been asleep too, somewhere out in the shadows of Flip's "Crib".

Shit.

I had hoped to go ice fishing today.

"Time to get up fucker, it's Christmas," Jorge whispered.

"Come outside and see what Santa got for you."

Jorge must've decided I wasn't going back to sleep, so he left. It took me a moment to find my T-shirt and shoes, but I followed quickly. I was pretty sure I knew what Santa had brought.

Still blinking to adjust to the bright sunlight, I found Jorge waiting impatiently by a red Mercedes. He beamed with pride as I approached. As soon as I was there, he opened the trunk.

Crumpled up inside was a miserable suit, bound at the wrists. Michael Simons's eyes widened in recognition when he saw me, despite my newly blond hair. I don't know who he expected, but it certainly wasn't me.

"Good to see you again, Mr. Simons," I said cheerfully. Then turning to Jorge I asked, "Where are we going to dump his body?"

I slammed the trunk closed, and Jorge fell over in pantomimed laughter.

Deciding to let Simons stew a bit, I made my way up the rusty stairs and back into the warehouse hallway, with Jorge close behind.

The corridor let out into the same cavernous room that, less than twenty-four hours earlier, had been a dance floor. A half dozen skylights lit the room well, but revealed no trace of the previous night's festivities: gone were the crushed plastic cups, cigarette butts, vomit, spent balloons, and other debris. The eyes might be fooled, but there was no deceiving the nose.

Flip and Clyde were removing products from shopping bags and sorting and stacking them on a makeshift table built from sawhorses and plywood.

Clyde looked up and grinned wearily. "'Bout damn time, lazy ass."

"Yeah, I was beat," I said quietly. I surveyed the table: countless boxes of aluminum foil rolls, a dozen multimeters,

153

remote controls, a glue gun, a soldering iron, and numerous other electronic odds and ends. "You guys have been busy."

"We got everything on your list, bro," Flip said. "The old guy at Decatur Hobby thought we were setting up a major electronics manufacturing operation. He practically offered me a night with his wife if we sourced the rest through him. For an old bag, she was kinda hot."

I laughed, despite my mood. "Let's go ahead and get all the battery packs charging."

"Dude, what do you think we've been doing?" Clyde shot back irritably, pointing to the floor beneath a table. Leaning over, I could see rows of plugged outlets. "While you and your lady been getting a beauty rest, we've been doing all the work."

Before I could reply that Jessica was not my "lady," Flip spoke up. "There's coffee and food over there," he said, directing my attention to a cluster of bags and cups on the bar. "But I need my computer, man. Go wake up your girlfriend first."

"Come on! She's not my—"

"Check that shit, I got dibs on princesita," said Jorge. "¡Ella tiene buen culo!"

"Well, Jorge thinks the 'little princess has nice buns' so I guess you're too late, Books." Flip laughed. "I wish I got half the action Don Juan Kemo-San gets."

"Seriously, man. Why ain't you hittin' that?" asked Jorge. "If she looked at me like she does you, I'd'a done been round them bases a few times."

"Kemo, why don'tcha do something useful?" suggested Clyde. "We need some music."

That rang Jorge's bell. As he made his way toward the DJ booth, Clyde yelled after him, "None of that Bankhead rap, man. If you even think about playing that crap, I'll put a boot up your ass."

154

As I finished extracting the last of the multimeters from the packaging and began extracting a soldering iron, I wondered what Jorge saw in the way that Jessica looked at me. Whatever she may have thought of me forty-eight hours ago, she certainly knew the ugly truth now: Dale Adams was nothing but poor white trash, disguised only by a thin layer of education.

Stevie Wonder's "Isn't She Lovely" began playing at an earsplitting volume. Clyde cursed a blue streak, but eventually shook his head and shrugged his shoulders with acceptance. Apparently he figured this was better than the alternative.

It must be after noon, probably closer to one. Jessica had had several hours of sleep. I placed the new soldering iron on the table and decided it couldn't be delayed any further. We really needed Flip on the computer.

Jorge killed Stevie and I braced for whatever punishment was coming next. Suddenly the distinctive southern rock acoustic twangs of Drivin N Cryin's "Straight to Hell" filled the cavern. Jorge came out of the booth triumphantly. Clyde held a fist out patiently, head tilting back and forth to the rhythm, as Jorge sauntered across the room, delivering a bump on the way past.

"I grew up just west of the tracks," Flip sang out. I cracked up. By the time he got to the second verse, Jorge and Clyde had joined in. "She said, 'Son won't you go outside? I've a got a man coming over tonight. The seventh one in seven days'…"

All three of my brothers were singing at the tops of their lungs. Jessica could wait.

I picked up a screwdriver and, using the handle as a mic, belted out a mostly accurate version of the lyrics. Damn, it felt good. For the first time in days, my soul was completely unburdened.

The song had already been old when I was a kid, and

it'd been years since I'd heard it, the last time being around two a.m. at a high school party in Doraville. Two thirds of the underage drinkers had scattered when the police had finally decided enough was enough. But about fifty of us, those who'd been unlucky enough to have been inside when the cruisers arrived, were stuck. Somebody locked the doors and the cops were outside banging on windows and doors with increasing irritation. Clyde had cranked up "Straight to Hell" and the whole house serenaded the cops. They must have thought it was funny—they didn't write any citations or cart anybody off. They just told us Flip's neighbors had had enough, so beat it.

"'Cause I'm going str-a-a-a-aight to h-e-e-e-ell," I crooned into the screwdriver as the song closed. I opened my eyes to find Jorge grinning at me, pointing toward the hall.

Looking up, I saw Jessica standing there: hands on her hips, laughter in her eyes, watching me make an ass of myself.

I nearly lost my breath, I was so stunned by her appearance. One of Flip's harem—"club groupies," as he called them—was a stylist at the Van Michael Salon in Buckhead. She'd been flattered when Flip had asked her for help with the clandestine mission of creating disguises. She'd dyed my hair in the bathroom beneath Flip's loft, then took Jessica back as I'd sprawled out on the couch to wait.

I must have passed out. My next memory was of Jorge sitting on me to wake me up. Jessica wasn't on one of the other couches when I'd gotten up, so I'd assumed Flip had done the right thing and given up his bed in the loft above the bathroom in the warehouse apartment.

Kermit had undergone a stunning transformation. Her long, brown hair was now short, chopped, and light red with blond streaks. It had been cropped unevenly, giving texture and attitude that hadn't been there before. Though it was an almost boyish cut, somehow she seemed to glow with

156

femininity. And she wore jeans; I'd never seen her in jeans before. They hung low and clung to her curves, revealing four inches of soft skin below her blouse.

The music had stopped and the room was now deafeningly silent.

Jessica's head tilted sideways and her brow went up. "Country music? Really?"

"Yeah, you ain't from these parts, sweetness," laughed Flip. "That's Kevn Kinney. He's about as country as Snoop Dogg."

Jorge let out low whistle. "D-a-a-amn girl! You lookin' yummy, mamacita!"

She blushed modestly, looking away. When those demure eyes came back up, they focused on me shyly, but with question. She wanted my opinion.

I nodded enthusiastically. "He's right! You look... wow!"

Damn, that was stupid. I could have said she was the most beautiful thing I had ever seen. I could have said the heavens were weeping with joy. I could have said... aw, screw it. I was too embarrassed to look up; my eyes were stuck on her feet. She was wearing spaghetti-strap sandals, framing a display of delicate little toes crowned with fading pink nail polish.

What the hell was wrong with me? If there was anything I could handle, it was women. This girl was *not* kryptonite. I wasn't exactly a legendary mac daddy like my Emory buddy Greg, but I'd known more than my share of sorority chicks. I could mac, for crying out loud. Who's the mac? I'm the mac. There was still time. I looked up... only to get lost in those big, brown eyes, which were still studying me with interest.

Again I drew a blank, and all I could manage was a gruff: "We've got a lot to do, so get a move on already."

Her brows furrowed, and the look of disappointment in her eyes made me want to turn the dial up on my skateboard and splatter myself all over the ceiling. What an idiot.

"Get some food first," suggested Flip as he headed toward the door of his living quarters, Clyde and Jorge close behind.

Thankful for the opportunity to recover, I led Jessica to the food on the bar and tried to be magnanimous as I laid out her breakfast choices. I sat down with her, and the two of us ate in silence. I busied myself stuffing down cold egg and sausage burritos—half because I was starved, half to prevent myself from talking—while she picked halfheartedly at a chicken biscuit.

"Do you really think they're going do it? Do you really believe they'll put fifty million dollars in your bank account?" she asked.

"No, probably not," I said, trying to cover my mouth. I continued chewing more slowly now, thinking. "Clyde seems to think they will, but I don't. And even if they do, they still want us dead."

Reading her expression, I added hastily: "It doesn't really matter, though. We're just buying time. Once we put the do-it-yourself directions out there, it's game over for those guys. They won't have any reason to kill us anymore."

She thought about this quietly, lifting the lids of the various drinks, trying to find one that suited her. Eventually she sniffed out an unsweetened tea. "How much time do you think we have?"

"Clyde says he told those cholos to get your car out of town and make sure it got found," I answered. I knew good and well how they were going to "make sure it got found," but it didn't seem necessary to tell her that at the moment. "Hopefully by now the whole world thinks we're in Tennessee."

Jessica seemed content with this.

"So are you still seeing Samantha?" she asked innocently.

"Samantha Cabrelle? How did you—?" I started to ask,

as she stuffed a large bite of chicken in her mouth. Why did I suddenly feel so much better? "No, that's over. She was fun and all, but she was too... I don't know. I—I'm..."

This is your opportunity! Say something great, man go for it! I leaned in while my mind raced to conjure up something spectacular. She looked up in confusion because I had stammered to a stop.

And then... I kissed her.

Right there in the middle of a miserable warehouse, I kissed a girl whose mouth was stuffed with chicken and biscuit.

And she didn't push me away.

Immediately she melted into me, and with her hands behind my head, pulled me off the stool. Her lips were warm and wet, a tad crumby, and tasted like chicken. But it was the most delicious kiss ever.

I was all in, but before the embrace could get really heated, she pushed away at my chest, holding up one finger as she quickly chewed and gulped tea.

Before we could resume, Jorge came tearing out of Flip's apartment, screaming at the top of his lungs. "You motherfucker! You motherfucker!"

He never even slowed down, and before I could move, he crashed headlong into me, smashing me against the bar. The air was knocked from my lungs, and I couldn't resist the assault as he flung me to the floor. I gasped for breath while the three-hundred-pound beast pounced on me.

"You motherfucker! You did it man, you fucking did it!" Jorge yelled into my face. "You did it, Books! I love you man, I love you!" He squeezed my cheeks between two beefy paws and tried to kiss me as I struggled. "We're rich, bro, rich!"

I rolled over and struggled to crawl away. Jorge grabbed me by the hips, pretending to violate me.

"Books didn't do squat," Clyde told Jorge, reaching out

and pulling me free. "All he wanted to do was run away," he reminded us. Then, in a nerdy voice: "'These guys are serious, fellas. Why, they even carry guns. We just need to run and hide.'"

Clyde was grinning from ear to ear. "I told you, Books. Maybe you think you're too good for us, but we get shit right every once in a while."

"They *paid* us?" Jessica asked incredulously.

Instead of answering, Jorge scooped her up and waltzed around with her like she was an oversized doll.

I looked at Clyde seriously. He nodded with a sly smile. He put his arm over my shoulder as we watched Kemo's antics.

"Thanks, brother," Clyde said quietly. "Now we all have a ticket out."

This was great news. I just wished it could have waited for a couple more minutes.

Chapter 15
IN A HANDBASKET

"Thirty percent!" I all but shouted, incredulous. "Fifteen million bucks? You gotta be shitting me!"

Flip shook his head calmly. "Come on, man. I called in some big chips to get this done. You have no idea—"

"Tell 'em hell no!"

Flip stared at me blankly. The money was gone already. I thought about strangling him.

"This is *my* world," Flip snapped. "You need to trust that, brother. I know exactly what I'm doing. Thirty ain't that bad, considering." Flip stared hard at me, trying to force me to see the truth in his eyes. Finally he grinned. "The glass is always half-empty with you, bro. Instead of bitching about the price tag, you should be happy, like Jorge and Clyde."

"Dude, I'm not an ignorant ass like—"

"Fuck you," he said quietly. "You think you're too good for us."

"That's not what—"

"Motherfucker, I'm just as educated as you are. I was one semester short of graduating at MIT. I had an invitation to Stanford for grad school." He saw the change in my expression. "That's right, post-grad at Stanford. Maybe Clyde and Jorge can't appreciate that, but you know what time it is. You need to stop condescending like we're a bunch of ignorant hicks."

"Look—"

"Maybe you've changed," he said, coolly. "But *I* still know who my family is."

"Look, all I'm saying is it's a lot of money."

"For your edification," Flip said slowly, enunciating deliberately, "your money is now in the laundry. It's currently in the spin cycle, bouncing from bank to bank, Europe to the Caribbean to Asia, getting divided into smaller and smaller chunks. In a couple of days it will vanish completely through peer-to-peer exchanges, only to—" He paused, happy to see the surprise in my eyes. He misread it as confusion. "Peer-to-peer, meaning digital currency. Greenbacks becoming ones and zeroes. Think Bitcoin. After that, the money rinses out through millions of microtransactions, eventually coalescing into four numbered accounts in Hong Kong, tax free."

"Damn," I said quietly, surveying the monitors on his desk. Three smaller screens displayed closed-circuit live views of the warehouse, but a larger one displayed ever-changing charts and moving graphs, market indexes with tickers at the bottom. Another had financial forms waiting to be filled out, a Scottsdale logo at the top. Day trading?

Flip's tone softened. Clearly he saw that I was impressed. "That's just personal stuff," he said, gesturing at the screens. "I'm long on some options I played last week, before all the shit hit the fan. I was planning to sell out tomorrow, but this Friday is a triple witching. I'm enough in the black to cover my fees so I was going to go ahead and get out, in case we get too busy for me to keep an eye on the market."

"Sorry about that," I said sincerely. My life was bleeding misery, poisoning everyone I touched. "But why are you buying near-term anyway, especially so close to expiration?"

"Finally! Somebody I can talk to! Dude, I've missed you so much," Flip said, grinning happily. Then he shrugged. "I like the volatility. If you time it right, you can make a killing. This shit's more fun than Vegas."

I shook my head slowly.

"Look, you're right," Flip admitted. "Thirty points is high. Typically I clean my own money, usually costs about seventeen. But that's with a network of corporations already in place, plus my money starts as cash. So my seventeen is nothing but fees. Your money will benefit from scale, but the routine I put it through is far more complex than what I do with my own money. I have a buddy in Munich handling this for me. This guy is badass, I mean sick, bro." He paused and studied me somberly. "You know why I'm using him? Ain't 'cause I'm lazy."

"Then what gives?" I asked, brow furrowed.

"Dale," he said, using my real name, which was something he never did. "You've stirred up some very, very serious people."

"I know. I tried to explain that to Clyde. He—"

"Do you really? Do you really know what kind of people they are?" Flip asked, studying me skeptically. He held up a piece of paper with my handwriting on it: a list of Treadwell's venture capitalists. "With the exception of the old guy in the trunk of my car, every single name on this list is dead, all in one week. Suicide, heart attack, carbon monoxide, mugging, house fire, car accident. Most of these people are fairly high-profile. Yet there's barely a whisper in the media? Tell me, smart guy, who can do something like that?"

More death. I felt very heavy. The weight only grew as he explained the level of skill that had been unleashed online after he had posted my video demanding the ransom.

"This is a losing battle for us," Flip concluded. He handed me another piece of paper. "You've got the money in your hands. You've got the girl. I have plenty of cash and a fast car. My buddy Rafael has a boat. We could be in Miami in twelve hours, Havana three days later. A little paperwork, then off to Hong Kong." He smiled, nodding victoriously at me. "Dude, we could be chillin' with mai tais on the beach in Thailand by next Thursday!"

And there it was: a way out. The more I thought about it, the better it sounded.

"Fuck that," I heard myself saying. "I want my life back. I want my name. I want that fucking paper from Emory. I want my fucking future."

"What are you, stupid?" Flip was furious. "Did you not just hear what I told you? There is no way we—"

"But we got Simons, didn't we?" I pointed out. "I want my life back."

"Your *life?*" he asked, incredulous. "Jesus Christ! We're *Doraville boys*. Get that through your skull. Take the money and run, bitch!"

He was right and I knew it. But I found myself saying, "Let's talk to Simons."

* * *

What the hell was Jorge doing in the hallway? He was supposed to be distracting Jessica out in the club "Cavern" of the warehouse. Jorge waved madly for us to hurry on past. But too late—the bathroom door opened, and Jessica came out.

"Oh my God!" she shrieked, immediately recognizing the disheveled man that Clyde was escorting down the hallway.

Simons looked up. He stared hard at Jessica, and suddenly his expression changed. "Hey, you're that... that pool girl? I know you!" Simons laughed. "Great. I've been kidnapped by a band of idiots."

Once again I was at Emory, waiting to go in and deliver my skateboard pitch, and Jessica was coming down the hallway, nose in the air, tears streaming down her cheeks after pitching her idea for a company that delivers blocks of ice to cool pools. I felt like punching Simons.

Instead I grabbed his shoulder and tried to push him through the door into Flip's apartment. He resisted by going limp, collapsing to his knees.

"Get her out of here," I growled at Jorge.

"You're in big, big trouble, missy," Simons told Jessica. "I don't know how you got mixed up in this, but you better go call the police. Now!"

Clyde and Flip were dragging Simons across the floor.

"I thought you said we weren't going to kill anybody!" she screamed from the hall as I slammed the door.

Simons was looking up at me, eyes wide. "Wait! You don't have to kill anybody."

"Right, civilized people shouldn't kill other civilized people, should they?" I asked. Clyde had cut the ties from Simons's wrists and propped him up on a chair. "Tell that to Keith Evans. Or Dr. Prestone. Or Terry Johnson and Stanley Philips. Mrs. McKinzie? And I really liked Mr. Treadwell, you asshole. Why the fuck did you have to kill his wife, too?"

I was furious. Too furious to notice the change in his expression.

"That's just a start, motherfucker!" I yelled, as Clyde pushed me back. "What about those cops? The innocent people at the gas station?"

Simons's eyes hardened. "I don't have to talk to you. We're all dead anyway."

As I struggled for control, Flip asked a question that stopped me dead. "What you mean 'we,' paleface?"

"Oh come on, think about it," Simons said, exasperated. He was rubbing his wrists. "I'm just a loose end, no different than you."

Clyde released me. I pushed him away. Simons was a loose end?

"But," I said slowly, thinking, "it's *your* people behind all the killing."

"Maybe," he answered, quietly. Then he added, "Yes, probably. But so what?"

"So what?" I repeated, confused. "You're the chairman of the board. That puts you in charge."

Simons laughed. "Please. I'm nobody."

"No, you're not," I insisted. "How does a *nobody* put fifty million in my bank account?"

Simons was clearly shocked. He thought about it for a moment, then shrugged. "It's just a distraction. You won't live long enough to see a penny of it."

I knew that already, so no surprise there. Although I didn't enjoy hearing him say it, especially in such a matter-of-fact tone. What *was* surprising, however, was his genuine shock about the exchange of money.

"So you're in control of the organization, but you're not in the loop about what they're doing," Flip said, voicing the question that was in my head.

"You just don't get it," Simons said, shaking his head with frustration. "I'm not in charge of anything. I'm a nobody with a do-nothing job. I'm just public relations. Treadwell asked me to sit in on his class presentations. That was a good fit for what I do, so I went. Then some kid," he said, turning his hand over, indicating me with his palm up, "goes floating around the room on a magical skateboard, talking about batteries that last forever. Personally, I thought the whole thing was some kind of scam, just a really good magic show. But I passed the information along." He paused, looking around. "I just raised a flag, that's all."

Shit. This wasn't going well. "So if it's not Greener

Georgia that's behind all this, then who? Who did you 'raise a flag' for?"

Simons was quiet for a long moment. When he finally spoke, it made no sense. He shook his head sadly and said, "Charon."

"Charon? What is Charon?" I asked.

Again he was quiet for a long moment. "My wife died eight years ago. I have two daughters, and they haven't spoken to me since the day of the funeral. Charon was all I had."

"I'm sorry your wife died," I said softly, trying to sound sympathetic. "But that was eight years ago." My tone hardened again. "Welcome to today, my friend. We're in a bit of a mess here and you're the one that caused the whole damn thing. Please pull your shit together and give us something we can use."

"Treadwell's wife. Her name was Charon," Simons said bitterly, wringing his hands. "She was my sister."

We were all stunned.

I felt nauseated. This blubbering mess was supposed to be the key to turning the tables. But he was a nobody? If it wasn't Greener Georgia behind all the chaos, then who?

"I'm really sorry to hear that," I said quietly. "But... please, who's behind this? Who did—"

"I killed my own sister," he said, staring at his hands.

"No, you didn't. You just 'raised the flag', right? *They* killed Charon, not you. You didn't know they were going to do that, right? Tell us who they are—help us get to them."

Simons looked up and stared blankly at the wall. "It doesn't matter. I'm dead. You're dead. Everybody's dead. It's a machine. It can't be stopped."

Shit. I felt each word as a dagger.

Suddenly Simons's eyes focused. On me. "You seem like a good kid. You're definitely brighter than I gave you credit for. How did you get them to give you money?" Simons

167

asked. But his curiosity was gone before I could answer. "No matter. You want to know about Greener?"

"Not really. I want to know who you called."

"NTD," he said. "Greener's New Technologies Division. That's who I called."

I waited, but no further explanation came. "I don't understand. You guys—"

"The whole thing is a sham," Simons said. "Greener Georgia, Greener Florida, Alaska, California, New York, and so on. Then there's the European, Asian, African chapters. We have a presence in pretty much every fuel-consuming or fuel-producing nation in the world. Our stated goal is to find and fund energy conservation initiatives. And that's exactly what we do." He paused, considering his words. "We fund wind farms, ethanol producers, solar panel campaigns, and pretty much any other non-fossil-fuel technologies that have no hope of making a real difference. And of course we're concerned about the local environment, so we back those who fight against nuclear power, and support conservationist groups who don't want to see their favorite river getting damned up for hydroelectricity."

Simons was smiling to himself, thinking aloud. "It really is a beautiful retirement package, becoming chairman of the board for Greener. Retiring politicians get cushy book deals or do-nothing consulting gigs. But oil execs go to Greener— and get to rewrite their legacy." He laughed. "Everybody loves Greener; we fight for the environment. I'm the toast of the town."

He smiled crookedly, his eyes bitter. I almost felt bad for him.

"And, in the event that we come across something truly unique," he said, looking at me, "we're supposed to write it up and send it to the NTD in Seattle. So that's what I did."

I waited for more. None came.

"So… this NTD," I said slowly. "They killed everybody?"

Simons shrugged. "Probably."

"So who are the other guys?" I asked. "The last time somebody took a shot at us, another group interfered and saved us. We got away while everybody was shooting at each other."

Simons's brow was up, but he didn't seem surprised. "That was your ticket out, your only hope."

"Who are they?"

"How should I know?" Simons asked, shrugging. "Illuminati, Freemasons, Skull and Bones, Bilderberg Group? It's just *They*. Until today, I just thought *They* were a product of brandy snifters and stale cigars, long clubhouse nights. *They* are nothing more than the meanderings of tired old men. Greener is the real God."

"And God is going to kill you?"

His answer came more slowly this time. "Yes. It seems logical. I asked for a more serious security detail, but they left me with my usual guy. That's when I knew I was going to die. This morning I thought *he* was there to do the job," Simons said, nodding at Clyde. "But now I know the truth. I was just bait. Bait doesn't need security. They'll kill me when they kill you."

Alarm bells were going off in my head. Simons was way too resigned to his destiny.

"We took care of them," Clyde spoke up. "Two guys in a blue Chrysler. Kelner wiped 'em out on 285."

Simons shook his head slowly. With certainty.

"*I'm* dead. *You're* dead. We're *all* dead," Simons predicted quietly. He nodded at Clyde but spoke to me. "You need better help."

Simons reached into his pocket quickly, pulling something out before any of us could get to a gun.

It wasn't a weapon.

It was a cell phone.

"Oh fuck," Flip yelled, snatching the phone out of Simons's hand and dashing it to the floor.

"Monitors! Check the monitors!"

"Relax," Clyde said, calmly. "I can see 'em from here. I've been watching the whole time."

"We need to get the fuck out of here," Flip said, not nearly as calm as Clyde. "Go get Jorge and Jess from the Cavern."

Clyde was annoyed. "Nobody's getting in this place. We've got cameras on every door, booby traps at every point of—"

"They're coming," Simons said quietly. "We're all dead. I'm dead, you're—"

"Shut the fuck up," Clyde snapped. "Fine. I'll go get 'em. But if we leave, we'll be exposed. What was the point of turning this place into a fortress if we ain't gonna use it?"

I fished the pistol Clyde had given me out of my bag and tucked it behind my back. As Clyde left the room, I turned to Flip. "He's got a point. We've got this place sewed up."

Flip glanced over his shoulder. He was kneeling in front of a safe. "You really think a few booby traps are gonna slow these guys down? I don't care what you say, we're going to Miami."

Shit. Flip realized his mistake as soon as I did. Simons was rocking back and forth, mumbling to himself. But surely he'd heard that.

Flip threw a black bag onto the table next to the remotes. He nodded at Simons and raised his brows. I shrugged. I didn't know what do with him either.

"Fuck is that?" I asked about the bag.

Flip grinned. "Toothbrush, toothpaste, change of underwear, little bit of cash. My 'go bag.'"

I eyed the remotes, twelve of them, lined up on the edge of the table in front of the computer, labeled to correspond with the videos. We'd spent all afternoon covering the insides of doors with aluminum foil and rigging them to my gravity devices. If some unfortunate fuckers rang the back door, a press of a button would launch the door straight at them. Make it into the hall, an aluminum covered board would splatter someone into the ceiling.

Clyde was taking his sweet time. I could see him having a silent conversation with Jorge and Jessica on one of the monitors.

"If you're ready, let's just go," Flip said.

"Yeah," I agreed. I turned to Simons. "You! Get up. We're going to leave you in the bathroom."

"No! Please don't leave me! Please," Simons begged.

"Get up," I demanded.

"Sweet Jesus," whispered Flip.

Flip's heads-up was followed by a loud thud against the wall, despite the soundproofing. As the smoke cleared, the live feed showed Clyde, Jorge, and Jessica all crumpled on the ground. A grenade?

How the...

And there it was, a perfect plan gone to complete shit. Two masked men, swinging down from the skylights. *Skylights*. The fucking skylights.

And then I was in motion, running for the only door out of the apartment. The gun was in my hand. I had to help. I had to do something.

"Wait!" It was Flip. "Look at this! We have to—if you go out, earplugs!"

I hesitated, digging in my pockets. That was enough of a pause to get me thinking. I ran back.

"Oh, Jesus," Flip moaned quietly. Every screen was populated with armed men.

Flip turned to the table and grabbed a remote.

"Wait," I said, grabbing his arm. I released him and ran for the door. Over my shoulder I yelled, "Wait till I'm out the

171

door, then blow 'em all!"

And then I was in the hall, running. A great gust of wind pulled and then shoved me, propelling my body into the great room like a rag doll. I tumbled and tumbled. And stopped.

I was on top of somebody. He was wearing a mask; his mouth was moving. But if he was saying anything, I couldn't hear it.

The world was coming back into focus. I'd lost my pistol, but there was a gun under the man. Some kind of assault rifle. I took it.

Clyde. So fucking dead. Blood everywhere, red bubbles gurgling out of his mouth. Jorge was bleeding, too. From the chest.

Shit. I was on my knees when my senses came back. I stood up. There was only silence, except Jorge's gasping. And car alarms outside.

Where was Jessica? Her foot was dangling out from under the board we had been using as a workbench earlier. I threw it off of her. She was unconscious, but I couldn't any find any serious signs of trauma. She wasn't dead.

"Get up," I said, shaking her urgently. "Please, you have to wake up! Get up!"

Ow! Shit! What the fuck? I was suddenly on the ground again, my back hurting like a motherfucker. Flip was standing over me, pointing his gun at something. He squeezed off three rounds in quick succession.

I stood back up again, but it wasn't easy. My legs were weak. Flip was pushing me down the hall. I could hear gunshots. Lots of them. Everywhere, except inside.

"Go, go, go! Move!" Flip was yelling. He scooped up two bags in the hall and handed them to me. "Carry this!"

Outside, there were bodies scattered everywhere. I stumbled down the steps, and Flip opened the door on the Mercedes, grabbed the bags from me, and dropped them in

172

the trunk. It was dusk, but still very bright. The gunshots were reaching a crescendo out on the street—sustained bursts from fully automatic weapons. An even more distant battle seemed to be going on somewhere else. The sky?

"What the fuck are you waiting for?" Flip asked, staring at me from the back of the car.

"We can't go," I said simply.

Flip shook his head slowly. He leveled his gun at me. "Get in the motherfucking car or I will drop your ass right here. Jorge is dead. Clyde is dead. And fuck that stupid bitch; we don't even know her."

We had a staring contest. "We're not leaving her," I said quietly.

His lips were tight, his teeth clenched. Finally: "Fine. Fucking fine. Just wait in the fucking car. I'll—"

"I'm coming—"

"No you're not," he yelled angrily. "You've been shot, dickhead."

I saw the butt of his gun just before it caught my temple.

Chapter 16

REFUSAL OF BOON

I t was bright. Really bright. I blinked, trying to focus on the face that was two inches from my nose.

"He's awake."

A man's face. Blue paper cap. A doctor? He looked familiar.

"Where's Jessica?" I croaked.

He glanced off to the side. After a moment, I heard a quiet reply. Flip's voice. "I tried, brother. I tried. Took a bullet, trying."

No. Shit.

"I was a few years ahead of you guys, so you probably don't remember me," said the doctor. "But you used to date my—"

"Jimbo," I said, closing my eyes.

Isn't he an animal doc? I thought to myself as light faded to dark.

* * *

I was in a bed. Daylight streamed through the windows. As I struggled to orient myself, my mind presented an image of Clyde and Jorge, mortally wounded, lying in pools of blood. Jorge gasping like an animal.

Fuck, Flip had failed to save Jessica. Or did I dream that part?

I sat up. Or I tried, anyway. Crippling pain shot up from my back.

"Oh shit! For crying out loud!"

I was cursing furiously when the door opened.

"Just relax, man," Flip said. "Don't try to get up yet. Jimbo says—"

"Where are we?"

"Macon. Jimbo has a veterinary practice down here. We're at his house."

Macon, Georgia. About an hour south of Atlanta. Flip was on crutches; his left leg was bandaged.

"You got shot?"

"Yeah, man," he answered quietly. "You wanted Jessica, so I went back for her. She was alive. Didn't look like she was hurt bad, but she was out. I was dragging her out when... well, shit got crazy, bro. I'm sorry, man."

I closed my eyes. What the hell was the point of all this? Why did they have to kill her? And Jorge, and Clyde?

"You're a hero again," Flip said. "And so is Clyde."

That didn't make any sense. I ignored it. "How bad's your leg?"

He gave a crooked smile. "Worse than you. Jimbo says I need surgery, a procedure he's not equipped for. But yours went right through, didn't hit any organs. You had some internal bleeding, though. Jimbo patched you up, says you just need some rest. You've been sleeping for two days."

Shit. Two days? Jessica's fate was sealed, then. No going back. Nothing could be done.

"Clyde's a hero?"

"Yeah," he answered, shaking his head slowly. He held up a newspaper. "He's a 'drug dealer with a love for America.'

175

Apparently he tipped off authorities to a terrorist cell that was financing its operations by dealing drugs. He died leading Homeland Security agents to a warehouse on Samson Street. Forty-two dead, including Clyde. Three in a helicopter that got shot down."

A cover-up. Forty-two dead?

Flip went on to explain that the firefight outside of the warehouse had been a far larger event than what had been visited upon us inside. In fact, it had become a rolling gun battle that raged on for nearly an hour after we were gone. News channels had been broadcasting nonstop, throughout the event and ever since—including amateur footage of passing car chases and at least three videos of a helicopter spinning out of control, billowing black smoke as it came down like a rock.

"They're treating it like it's 9-11 again, 'America's under attack,'" he said, shaking his head. "And people are buying this shit. The really fucked-up thing? If I wasn't there—if I didn't know what *really* went down—I'd believe it, too! And since then, there's been a whole series of bombings and assassinations all over the world, all tied to this 'terrorist cell.' Then yesterday, two buildings blew up at the same time: one in New York, one in Seattle."

I was confused. It was one thing to cover up events in Atlanta, but what was all this other stuff? Was it related to us?

"I gotta piss like a mother," I said.

Flip grinned. He nodded at the nightstand beside me. "Just use that bottle. I'm outta here."

Beside the bed was a banana-shaped green tray and an opaque bottle with a wide mouth and curved neck.

"I ain't pissing in a bottle," I said, propping myself up on the bed, groaning.

"Chill."

I ignored him, gritted my teeth, and gingerly swung my

176

legs off the bed. Searing pain shot up my side as I pushed myself into a sitting position. It hurt something fierce, but it wasn't agony. I could manage this.

I pushed off the bed.

Flip stepped aside as I slowly approached. "First door on the left."

After handling my business, I examined myself in front of the mirror. I was wearing only boxers. A bandage was wrapped all the way around my abdomen. On my right side, additional square bandages were underneath the wrap. That was the real source of the pain; must have been where the bullet went through.

"Hungry?" Flip asked, standing in the doorway behind me. The word ignited growling hunger pangs in my stomach.

"Yeah."

"Go sit back down. I'll bring you something."

The pillows had been stacked up on the bed so I could sit. There was a refolded copy of the *Atlanta Journal* waiting for me. I spent the next fifteen minutes skimming through the coverage of all the terrorism.

Apparently Atlanta had been home to a cell of Ansar Al Jihad, an Al Qaeda affiliated group; the Atlanta cell had reportedly controlled US operations.

Though the battle in Atlanta had foiled a local plot, bombs had gone off in New York and Seattle, killing one hundred seventy-three. Similar bombs had gone off in London, Paris, Jerusalem, Cairo, and Dubai. But unlike 9-11, these attacks hadn't been focused on killing ordinary civilians—rather, they had targeted oil companies and executives. Ansar Al Jihad had released a video through Al Jazeera, accusing these companies of funding a war against the Quran.

There was a two-page article laying out Clyde's entire life, heralding him as a hero who had saved hundreds of lives. I was surprised to learn that his father, the man I had known my whole life as an ultra-pious patron of God, had once done an eight-year spin for involuntary manslaughter. An incident that had occurred as a teenager.

But there was no mention of Jorge. And the only mention of Jessica was buried in a small article in the Metro section, a story about the Atlanta police retracting the warrants for our arrests in connection with bank robberies. Apparently a lab tech had misfiled fingerprints from a gas station robbery.

In an unrelated blurb, Michael Simons had been killed in a botched robbery.

Flip hobbled in on one crutch, a plate in his free hand. It was piled high with scrambled eggs, bacon, and toast. He looked on as I attacked it like a starving cat.

"So I've been thinking," he said quietly. "Even though your name is cleared, they're still looking for you. I haven't released that how-to video for making your gravity board yet. Nor any of the other stuff."

I paused in my chewing. He was right. Clearing my name did little to improve my situation. There were still those who wanted me dead.

"If we release the video," Flip continued, "then there's no reason to kill you. At least, I can't think of any." He scratched the back of his head. "But I still think we should jet, just lay low for a while. Your money is still in process, but it's going smooth, should be available in a few days. I reached out to my buddy Rafael. Miami is good to go."

I processed this, while Flip watched me closely. I gulped some milk, washing down the last of the toast. "Yeah, I think you're right. Don't post the video yet, though. I want to think things over."

* * *

The trip to the restroom had caused some red blotches

to appear on my bandage. I spent the rest of the day in bed. But the next morning I felt much better and refused to stay in that bed a moment longer, no matter how badly Jimbo wanted me to. But I did agree to take it easy, and lounged in front of the TV all day.

By Sunday I was feeling really good, even without painkillers. Flip, on the other hand, was in a lot of pain. A tendon had been severed and, according to Jimbo, needed to be pulled out and reattached. Flip insisted he could wait, and have it looked at in Cuba where it could be done anonymously.

According to the news, the fear of any more immediate terrorist attacks had subsided a bit, but the US had nevertheless strengthened its fleet in the Persian Gulf, which in turn had sparked Iranian threats against traffic in the Strait of Hormuz. Negotiations at the United Nations had taken center stage.

And though I pored through everything I could find about the incident at the warehouse, it became clear that nobody gave a shit about Jorge Ortiz. Not a single mention whatsoever. I thought about his poor, sweet mother, and all her huge spaghetti dinners when we were kids. And the Wee Tea! How we loved that disgustingly sweet tea: basically pure sugar, flavored with a bit of tea. We called it Wee Tea because it ran right through you. I wondered what she was thinking. I wondered if Jorge's body had turned up somewhere. Was the Ortiz home a place of grief and sorrow? Or was Jorge's mother sitting and waiting for news of her son—news that would never come?

At least Clyde was a hero. If you gotta go, what better way? I watched his father being interviewed on CNN. His chest swelled with pride, even as bitter tears rolled down his cheeks. Clyde may have had his troubles, but now he was a true American hero who gave his life for our country.

It was all so pointless. All these deaths... and they were

my fault. *I'd* killed everyone, same as if I'd pulled the trigger myself. How had I gotten Jessica into this mess? Why did I bring the whole thing to Doraville? What a punk. I'd brought this rain of shit down on everyone I loved.

And it was all over nothing. Well, not nothing: Over *money*. Over *power*. These motherfuckers killed my family over some... I don't know. And then they used the whole thing to carry off some fucked-up agenda. To accomplish what?

Who fucking cared? These fuckers needed to be stopped.

And *I* could stop them.

I stubbed my cigarette angrily in the ashtray. Flip, who had been lying back on a deck chair with both hands behind his head, peered at me through his sunglasses.

"I'm going back," I announced.

He was quiet for a moment. "You can't do that, man. Tomorrow morning, we're going to Miami. By the time we get there, our video will have propagated onto thousands of servers all around the world. We'll—"

"I'm going back. These guys need to go down."

"*Fuck* them! If you go, you die. And you have thirty-five million reasons to live, just waiting for you in Hong Kong."

Flip was quiet again. Then he added, quietly, "Look, you don't have to worry about Greener anymore, I think. And I'm pretty sure that as soon as that video gets released, you won't have to worry about *They* either."

"What? What do you mean I don't have to worry about Greener?"

He didn't answer for a long moment.

"Just wait here a minute," he said, struggling to get up. He hobbled inside on his crutch.

When he returned, he handed me a small laptop. He said nothing; just turned and plunked back down in his chair, stretching out again.

I opened the laptop. It wasn't password-protected. A

browser window was open on a YouTube video. *My* video: the one where I'd requested payment of fifty million dollars.

Beneath the video were two comments:

> **InterestedParty_ATL:** "Acknowledged."
> **InterestedParty_Eliminated:** "Greener days are gone, from New York to Seattle. But would still love to chat. Kermit misses you. You know where we are. Pass the word, Philip."

Kermit misses you.

"She's alive! You motherfucker! How long have you known about this?"

"She's alive? What the fuck are you talking about? Look at the last message. They know who I am! It says—"

"That's what I'm looking at!" I yelled. I was furious; just a breath away from bashing the laptop over his head. "It says Jessica is alive!"

"What the...?" he trailed off. "It doesn't say anything about Jessica. It says that they took out Greener, 'from New York to Seattle.' You remember that Simons said Greener's New Technologies Division was in Seattle? So this must be a post from the other guys, the ones that Simons said were make-believe. They're saying those bombings in Seattle and New York took out Greener."

"Kermit," I said, more calmly now that I realized he'd had no way of knowing. "Kermit is Jessica's nickname. They must have her."

We were both quiet. My mind was racing.

"Fuck. I didn't know, man. I just didn't want you to get all stirred up. You know it's just a trap."

"What do they mean?" I asked. "What makes them think I know where they are?"

"Peachtree-DeKalb Airport," he answered simply. "I'm pretty sure, anyway."

I was confused. And pissed. "How the hell do you know

181

that? And what the fuck else are you holding out on me?"

"Nothing, man, I swear," he answered. "You remember I told you they hit my trap right after I posted this video? Well, I hit 'em back. In the process, I traced their IP to a node at the airport."

"Gimme the keys," I demanded.

Flip refused, and we almost came to blows. Eventually, cooler heads prevailed, and Flip talked me off my impetuous ledge. I would still go to Atlanta—but I wouldn't go charging in there like a fool. We needed two days of preparation first.

Later that night, Flip had a member of his "digital brotherhood" access my YouTube account to post a reply: "Kermit likes to fly. Have a plane on the tarmac, Friday 5pm."

Chapter 17
DOWN THE MOUNTAIN

It was Friday. I checked my watch: 4:48 p.m.

I climbed out of the Mercedes. I was in a medium-sized parking lot populated by several dozen cars, with a clear view of a twin-engine Cessna taking off down the runway. Peachtree-DeKalb Airport is a small hub: just a couple buildings, a tower, and a few hangars.

A man on a golf cart approached. The man was so large that he dwarfed the cart, making it look like a tiny clown car. It was the man from Manuel's Tavern, the one that had been walking his dog.

"Mr. Adams?"

He knew good and well who I was. I climbed in and asked, "How's your girlfriend?"

He cracked a smile despite himself. "She's doing well. You can ask her yourself in a moment."

We rode along in silence. There wasn't a single soul in sight. He drove us through a gate and along a row of parked private planes, and eventually stopped by a small door on the side of a hangar. The big man climbed off and the suspension breathed a sigh of relief, lifting me a few inches.

He held the door for me. I walked through. And there was his girlfriend, replete with half a purple face. The swelling was gone and the bruise was healing, but the mark was still there.

"Shit. Sorry about that," I said, genuinely feeling bad about it.

She said nothing. They were both silent as she patted me down. Then the man opened another door into a hallway. He led me down the hall to the first door on the right, opened it, and stood back. I walked in, and the door closed behind me.

"Books! Fuck yeah!" Jorge rolled toward me on a wheelchair. He hugged my waist with one arm. "I knew you'd come back for us!"

I was completely stunned. "You... you're... you were dead! Oh, Lord Jesus! Thank you, Lord, thank you!" The relief was so overwhelming that I was nearly in tears as I squeezed Jorge's beefy neck.

Jessica quietly watched this reunion of brothers. She was much more reserved, but she was beaming. I smiled at her. "How are you, Kermy?"

So much for reserved. She all but jumped into my arms, hugging me and kissing my face over and over. "We thought you were dead! They haven't been telling us anything! Oh my God!"

"I take it you weren't too badly hurt." I grinned. "But you..." I turned to Jorge. "You were a wreck last time I saw you."

"Yeah, man. Collapsed lung. They say I gotta take it easy for a while," Jorge said. He studied me for a moment. "I don't know if you know it, but they got Clyde, man. He's dead."

"Yeah, I know. I saw him," I said, shaking my head sadly. We were both silent for a moment. But I didn't want to dwell on that now, so I quickly changed the subject. "So look, I'm gonna get you guys out of here. I have to—"

"A-hem!" Jorge interrupted me, clearing his throat and nodding up toward the corner. A camera.

184

"Yeah, I figured," I said. "As I was saying, I have to go talk to these people. And then we're leaving." I faced the camera, flipped a bird at it, and asked, "Y'all ready?"

The door opened again.

"Give 'em hell, Books."

I stepped into the hall. The big guy opened a door at the end. Out into a hangar—filled with desks, computers, and people. I could tell that, just moments before, the place must have been a hive of activity; but as we entered, all activity immediately came to a standstill. People were virtually frozen in place as all eyes turned to me. A phone rang, but no one answered.

I felt really strange with so many eyes on me, watching me in silence as I followed the giant man toward the middle of the hangar. But I supposed everyone knew who I was. They had all been spending their every waking moment searching for me. And now they were finally getting to see me. I bet they were disappointed that I wasn't more impressive. Just some dude in blue jeans.

The big man led me to the center of the hangar, where a semicircle of video screens had been arranged near a boardroom table. A portly man with frazzled white hair sat at the table alone, but rose from his chair as we approached, and stepped forward, his hand extended.

"Hi, I'm Nathan," he said warmly, shaking my hand. "Nathan Letson. But I'd rather you just call me Nathan. Can I call you Dale? Or do you prefer Books?"

I found myself a little put off by his overly friendly nature. I'm not sure what I was expecting, but it certainly wasn't this. "Dale will do."

"Dale it is," he said, smiling happily. "I'm so glad you decided to come in. I was really worried for a while there! Our forensic guys said you'd lost a lot of blood. There was a chance you were dead."

I said nothing. I had a job to do, but I was going to let him talk first.

It seemed that Letson wasn't a fan of silence. "But you're here! You're alive and well, thank God! And, as you can see, we have taken good care of your friends."

He waited, wanting me to acknowledge this. I waited, too.

"I was very, very sorry to hear about your friend Clydell," he said sincerely. The warmth in his eyes disappeared. "Those responsible have been *dealt with*."

A shiver ran down my spine. This guy was dangerous.

"And it won't ever happen again, to anyone, ever," he said, studying me.

This I wanted to know more about. "You're referring to the bombs in Seattle and New York? Cairo and Dubai?"

"Yes, yes. Those and a few other little things that didn't make the news. The Greener organization is no more. You have nothing to fear."

I smiled. *How dumb does he think I am?*

He read my mind. "Son, we are not your enemy," he said, with apparent sincerity. "We saved your life twice. You know I speak the truth. And we saved your friends. They were—"

"What the fuck do you want from me?" I said, cutting him off. Letson winced at my foul language. "You want the device, right? And if I don't give it to you, you'll kill us all. You can cut the nice-guy bullshit."

"We already have the device," he answered quietly. "You left several behind at your friend Philip's warehouse."

The booby traps. We'd built nine devices and had left them scattered about at the entrances, attached to remote controls. I'd been holding on to the slim hope that they hadn't been found and figured out.

"So we... we can go then? You're just going to let us walk right out?"

"Yes," he said, smiling. "Absolutely! We have a plane

waiting on the tarmac. It will take you and your friends anywhere you want."

I stared at him. There was a catch. There had to be.

"But we'd like to talk before you leave," Letson said. Reading my expression, he rushed ahead. "Just a few minutes of your time, that's all. You *are* free to go, honestly. But I have a proposition I'd like to make. It will only take a moment. Please give me that." He paused, seeing that I wasn't convinced. "Just think of it as payment for taking care of your friends."

He had me. If I walk, I'm an asshole. I wondered what would happen if I decided to just go ahead and *be* an asshole. Somehow I doubted I'd get far.

"I appreciate all that you've done for Jorge and Jess," I said. "Listening to your proposition is the very least I can do."

"Wonderful! I think you're going to love what I have to say," Letson said, rubbing his hands together. "We were very excited about your gravity device. And even more excited after our scientists had a few days to examine it." He studied me. "You've made a *major* technological breakthrough. This will change science forever; our physicists have confirmed it. Your name will go down in the history books as—"

"What's the proposition?"

He was displeased with my impatience, and struggled to hide it. "Yes. Well. You made a pitch before investors; that's what started all the killing. You want financial backing? Well, we want to give it to you." I had expected him to maybe offer to buy the device—not to form a partnership. He saw my surprise and was happy. "It gets even better! You'll retain one-hundred-percent control of all profits. We don't want any money."

"The catch?"

Letson looked at his hands for a moment, then back up again. "We'd like a seat at the table. We want to be involved in the planning. We need to help you control how this gets released."

I considered this. The one word that stuck out most was "control." These guys *were* in control. Of *everything*. And they wanted to *maintain* control.

"Thank you for your interest," I said. "But I've already received my seed capital. I'm no longer—"

"Yes, the fifty million on its way to Hong Kong," he said, smiling. "Keep it. Think of it as a signing bonus. Put *our* money to work, not yours. We can give you the top scientists in the world, the best engineers, the best programmers. When you're ready, we can set up factories, provide you with global logistics and distribution channels. You'll be the wealthiest man on the planet before you're thirty."

Fuck. That sounded good. All I had to do was sign. So why did I feel like I was talking to the devil?

"And if I say no? I can just walk out?"

"Yes."

"Okay, well do you have a card or something, in case I change my mind?"

His lips pursed, only for a moment. Then he shifted gears. "Don't you want to know why? Aren't you in the least—"

"I think I understand," I said.

He studied me quietly.

"This isn't about power," he said. "This is about order. This is about preventing civilization from slipping into chaos. You've been at Emory for the last four years, learning the basics of capitalism. Lecture after lecture on corporate finance, global markets, and so on. But you're inexperienced and… young. And the problem with being young is that you haven't yet realized you don't know everything. Why do you think Greener wanted you dead?"

That was easy. "Money. If the world has a cheap, infinite supply of power, say goodbye to fossil fuels. All their money

188

goes poof. Their children's children might one day have to get an actual job, God forbid."

"And why do you think we almost let them do it?" Letson asked. "Do you honestly believe you're the first person to ever come up with a viable alternative to fossil fuels? Why do you think that this time in particular we decided to intervene on your behalf?"

This was a more difficult question. "Because *you* wanted it? You wanted the technology."

"We have it already, so why are we talking?"

Back to an easy question. "Because you know if you kill me or my friends, how-to videos will get released on the Internet. The whole world will have access to the technology. Overnight there will be a changing of the guard, new wealth will be created, old wealth destroyed, and you'll be out of power. I've got you by the balls and you know it."

"You're partially correct. We have always been the keepers of order and we always will be," he said. "You're clearly a very bright young man, I must admit. However, you seem to lack the ability to see the full picture." He raised an eyebrow. "Who buys a gas-guzzling car when fossil fuels are obsolete? What happens to the workers when Ford and Chrysler close their doors on the same day? What about all the workers employed in upstream supply manufacturing? What about downstream distribution?"

He waited, but I didn't have an answer.

"I'm sure you've studied economies of scale," he said. "If you sell batteries that can power an entire home forever, those who can afford it will buy. But what happens on the day that most of the power company's customers disconnect, leaving only the poorest behind to pay for the costs of the old infrastructure? A zero will be added to those poor customers' one-hundred-fifty-dollar monthly power bills. They won't be able to pay it, and just like that, the system will collapse.

189

Overnight, millions will be without power. No food on the table because Dad just lost his job... and now no power. And millions more out of work because power lines don't need to be maintained, new wires don't need to be manufactured, service trucks don't need to be driven, built, or maintained."

He glared at me as if I were personally withholding food from some poor child.

"The effects would be devastating here in the US," he continued. "Yet they'd be far worse elsewhere, especially in third-world nations where workers already struggle. All we want is to ensure an orderly transition. To slow this thing down, and prevent an overnight meltdown of the civilized world. To mete it out carefully and allow change to occur in a gradual, controlled manner."

I thought about this. It was a lot to process.

"I guess I've been a little too busy over the last couple weeks to really think this thing through," I admitted. "But it seems to me that these things will take care of themselves. What if Henry Ford had decided not to create the assembly line because he didn't want to put horse ranchers out of business? What if electricity was shunned to prevent hardship on the families of candlemakers?" I paused, thinking. "I took a few history classes at Emory. You're right, I'm young. But one thing I do know: Every major shift in technology has resulted in an economic boom."

Letson looked angry; I suspected this wasn't going the way he had planned. He turned to the large man—who was still standing there, since he hadn't been dismissed. "Go get Dr. Stevenson," he demanded. Then he focused his glare on me. "You, son, are naively oversimplifying. While you are correct that there will be a boom, there will *also* be a *devastating* bubble before the diffusion. The effects on our society will be disastrous. This is much bigger than anything we've ever faced before. It isn't a mere 'shift' in technology. This is a revolution."

I tried to take this all in. "So, the reason you guys 'intervened'... was to prevent me from spreading the word? To stop me from bursting your little bubble?"

"No," he snapped. "You didn't make that threat until three days after we were already trying to find you. If all we wanted to do was stop you, all we had to do was let Greener carry out business as usual. Greener was a necessary evil; their greed maintained order, for better or worse. Normally, we—"

"That's him? Is that him?" I heard a voice behind us. A man walking fast, ahead of the big guy. "Oh my gosh, it *is* him! It's *you!* I'm so happy to finally meet you!"

The next thing I knew, a tall, lanky man in a tweed jacket was pumping my hand enthusiastically. "Hi, I'm Jacob! I'm really—I'm just so—this is great! I didn't think I was going to—"

"This is Dr. Jacob Stevenson," Letson interrupted. "Dr. Stevenson, meet Dale Adams."

"Jacob, call me Jacob," Stevenson said, still pumping my hand. "Mr. Adams, this is truly an honor!"

Who the hell was *this* clown? "Please, call me Dale. And may I have my hand back?"

"Oh, yes, certainly. I'm sorry."

All this civility was killing me. I was on a first name basis with all these assholes.

"Dr. Stevenson has been playing with your invention for the last few days," Letson explained. "And I would like for him—"

"It's not an invention, really," Stevenson interrupted. "Well, yes, the device itself is an 'invention.' But really, this is a *discovery!* A huge, gigantic, enormous, groundbreaking discovery! This is the most important discovery of—"

"Jacob," Letson said quietly. His tone stopped Stevenson. "Mr. Adams has refused my offer to finance the developing

191

of the technology. He's planning to walk out of here—and there's nothing I can do about it." He paused, turning to me. "Dr. Stevenson is the person who convinced the Order that you have something special. He's the reason you are alive today."

"The Order"? So "They" has a name?

"I have one final offer to make," Letson said. "But first, I ask that you give Jacob a moment to explain the reason we intervened. Then I will make my offer."

"That's it," I asked. "Listen to this guy, you make an offer, and I'm done?"

"That's it," Letson replied. He turned to Stevenson. "Go ahead, please. Explain the—"

"Where did all the videos go?" Stevenson asked, indicating the black screens in a semicircle before us.

Letson issued an order. The screens flickered to life, one by one. Suddenly I was seeing myself everywhere. The screens displayed the videos I had put up on YouTube so long ago. It felt like a lifetime had passed since then. I had just been chilling in my underwear, munching on some popcorn when I'd uploaded them. If only I could have imagined...

"Are you going to start, Jacob?" prodded Letson.

"Right, right, sorry! Okay, this whole thing is really astonishing," Stevenson began. "But your battery idea?" He pointed at the screen. "Talk about a stroke of genius! I mean, you just completely revolutionized—"

"Jacob!" snapped Letson loudly, causing Stevenson to nearly jump out of his tweed.

"Right. As fascinating as limitless energy might be to me, I'm sure the Order has warehouses filled with devices that are more efficient than fossil fuel," returned Stevenson with a touch of sarcasm, eyeing the puppet master. Letson simply ignored the accusation, and Stevenson continued. "The energy potential is, of course, transformational, but even if

192

we set that aside, there is yet *another* exciting possibility to consider.

"As I look at these videos I see the necessary ingredients to successfully execute a remarkable application. Let's start with this video"—he pointed to the screen that showed me riding the hoverboard—"where you demonstrate the basic ability to repel one mass away from another. What I see is the beginnings of an antigravity force field that could potentially deflect incoming masses. To test this, yesterday we took aluminum, wrapped it around a basketball, hooked it to one of the devices, and then turned it on." He leaned toward me. I could smell the coffee on his breath. "It was unbelievable! We couldn't hit it, crush it, or smash it! We even borrowed a weapon from one of the servicemen. The ball was impenetrable!"

I backed away, fearing spittle.

"Now, in this video"—he nodded at another screen—"we see a car being lifted off the ground. And yet both the board, and the aluminum under it, are not being crushed or broken to bits. We have calculated that the engine compartment weighs thirteen hundred pounds. But even though nothing is under that quarter-inch piece of plywood, it behaves as if it has the full support of a flat surface beneath it. What this implies is that the capacity to lift and support objects with very large mass is astoundingly high. In our experiments, we found that it's more than just a force like a magnet; it seems to be a conduit of *immense* energy. Something never observed by science before!"

He leaned back into my personal space, trying to infect me with his excitement.

"I'm sure you see where I'm going with this," Stevenson said with conspiratorial enthusiasm. I didn't bother telling him I had no idea where he was going with this. "This one discovery is the solution to many of the biggest challenges

193

facing space travel. You've provided the means to lift a super-large craft, say, the size of this hangar…" He gestured in a wide sweep, indicating the immense space around us. Then he pointed at the screen showing my paint can video. "And the means to get it out of the Earth's atmosphere without the need for millions of gallons of rocket fuel. And once in space, this very same phenomonon could be used to create Earthlike gravity to make the passengers comfortable—*all* with the vehicle wrapped in a protective shield that can deflect space debris!"

Stevenson stopped and beamed. He had been excited earlier, but now appeared ready to burst into confetti. "And here's the best part: what if a journey to Mars took only five minutes?"

Stevenson was shifting from foot to foot involuntarily, like a five-year-old with a secret.

"Gravity is fast—really fast! Nobody's certain how fast gravity propagates, but even the most conservative estimations put it at around the speed of light. General relativity suggests that the speed of gravity is limited to the speed of light, although other phenomena have brought that hypothesis into question. Yet even if we accept that the speed of gravity is finite and that travel must be limited to the speed of light, perhaps a mission in progress could travel at multiples of that speed by repelling off other objects traveling at the same *relative* speed! At least… theoretically." Stevenson smiled a bit self-consciously at this last.

"So my paint cans were leaving the Earth at the speed of light?" I asked, completely amazed.

"No, sorry, no. No way. That's not what I meant. You cans were tracked by JSpOC, a government agency that follows man-made space debris. They use phased-array radars to scan large areas in a fraction of a second. And even though these radars have no moving parts to limit the speed of the radar scan, it would have been impossible for them to have detected an object traveling at the speed of light. No, those paint cans were traveling at just over eighteen thousand miles per hour," answered Stevenson. "Actually, you're lucky you *didn't* achieve light speed. You would have been killed. The first paint can you sent up would have only made it a foot or two before creating enough friction to superheat the projectile and cause a major blast." He paused again, scratching his head. "We're pretty sure you were only playing around at the very bottom of the probable spectrum."

"I think that's enough, professor," said Letson. "Would you please explain the significance of what you're saying?"

"Why, yes, absolutely," replied Stevenson, smiling with renewed excitement. "Yes, this is a very significant development. It's potentially a huge technological leap for our space program. No, I'm sorry, no. Not a leap. It's more like primordial sludge evolving into *Homo sapiens* overnight, without need for millions of years of incremental steps! What you are looking at is an open door into a future only *dreamed* of by science-fiction writers. A way to make space travel as easy as going to the office—in our lifetime. A practical way to generate enough power to initiate terraforming on Mars, in the event humanity needed a new planet. A way to change the course of any large incoming asteroid pointed at Earth. Interstellar space travel at fast enough speeds to negate the need for theoretical flights of fancy, such as wormholes. And that's all after only a few days of playing with it!"

Stevenson paused and gathered control of his emotions. His next words were very calm, almost quiet. "You have made the greatest discovery of our lifetime. No, not just our lifetime. This is the single most significant scientific development in human history. This is the key to the future mankind *must* have."

"Dale," Letson said quietly. "You can go it alone, if you

insist. But we want time. We need time. Whatever you think of us, whatever you believe about us, you must know that we are benevolent caretakers. Hollywood has painted a grim picture of 'clandestine brotherhoods.' But we are not evil. It is our job to maintain order. That's all." He paused, staring at me earnestly, hoping I believed. "All I want is time. Let us figure this out before you start rolling out products that can be reverse-engineered and turned into weapons."

And there it was. My discovery could be used as a weapon.

"We will double what awaits you in Hong Kong," Letson said. "No, triple. Money is of no consequence. *Time* is."

I considered this. "How much time do you need?"

"Two years," he answered immediately. "Two years in a laboratory. In the meantime, you go on a vacation. Go to your graduation, then take a sabbatical. Hike the Alps, run with the bulls in Pamplona, take a spiritual quest to India. When you get back, do as you please, with no interference."

Stevenson was confused. "Two years is a long time! You can come work with me right now. I want to show—"

"Two years is a long time," I agreed. I glanced at my watch. "Can I have a few days to think about it? I have to check in soon or this entire conversation will be moot."

"Yes, absolutely," Letson said, breathing a sigh of relief. A "maybe" was better than a definite no. "We have a plane waiting on the—"

"I won't be needing the plane," I said. Letson's expression changed for a microsecond. "I'd like to collect my friends now."

* * *

Out in the parking lot, I watched as two men struggled to transfer Jorge into the Mercedes, then folded and loaded the wheelchair into the trunk. Jorge had a bag of meds on his lap.

I wasn't looking forward to getting him out of the car later, with only Jessica to help.

I checked my watch: 5:32 p.m.

As I turned left onto Clairmont Road, Jorge was the first to speak. "So, is that it? Is it over?"

"Almost," I answered quietly, checking the mirrors. I didn't see anybody, but I knew they were there.

We rode in silence for the next half mile. It was almost as if Jessica and Jorge were holding their breath. They knew something was up, but they were trying to let me concentrate. I mostly just didn't want to talk. Flip had warned me that they would probably bug the car. And I knew they'd kill us in an instant if I gave even the slightest hint of what I was planning.

I knew a terrible truth, but I couldn't share it. The only reason we were still breathing was because of Flip. But they were looking. It was only a matter of time. And once they found him, our defense would be undone. Nice-guy routine or not, Letson was efficient. And a zealot. No, he would never leave loose ends.

That left me only one solution.

On the other side of Buford Highway, I dipped into a parking lot and pulled up in front of an RV as large as a city bus.

"That's our ride," I announced. Flip had paid cash for it the day before.

"No shit! Awesome!" Jorge shouted his approval.

"What on earth?" Jessica asked, smiling crookedly, her brows raised incredulously.

"I'm serious," I said, smiling.

I opened the trunk, and Jessica watched as I unfolded the wheelchair.

"Help me get Jorge out? Pretty please."

Jorge was more helpful with us than he'd been with the

two men at the airport, but it was still a struggle. After much effort, we finally got him transferred into the RV.

The RV was the cheapest bus-style one they'd had on the lot, but it had still cost Flip a fortune. It was used, but in great condition. Jorge looked impressed as he slid into a booth with a table.

"Hey, waiter, we got anything to drink?" he asked. Jessica laughed, but I didn't crack a smile.

"Have a seat," I told Jessica, ignoring Jorge. Jessica slid in. "Buckle up, please."

Jorge laughed. "Still getting used to driving this beast?"

Again I ignored him, as I walked away. After a moment I returned with two full-faced motorcycle helmets. I only had the two. I hadn't anticipated Jorge being along for this ride.

I placed the helmets on the table in front of them. "Put them on, please."

I ignored their confused questions. Returning to the front, I strapped myself into the captain's chair. In the middle of the console was a bucket that I had screwed into the plastic housing. Inside were five remote controls with white labels and red markings: "Front"; "Back"; "Left"; "Right"; and "Up".

I picked up the remote labeled "Up."

"Hey, man, you're freaking me out, bro. Did you forget to take your meds? Why do we need—?"

Jorge's question was cut off by the sudden movement of the RV. Butterflies swooned in my stomach. It was a lot like going down a steep hill on a roller coaster. Only we had rocketed *up*, not down.

"Holy mother of shit! Jesus H. Christ! Holy son of a fucking cow! What the shit! I'm gonna—!" Jorge's rant suddenly gurgled to an abrupt conclusion.

Outside the window, the cars below looked tiny. I could see Clairmont Road, Buford Highway, and I-85. Friday afternoon rush. All six northbound lanes were gridlocked.

"Hey, um, little help please? Jorge threw up back here," Jessica pleaded. "And I think he passed out."

We were rotating slowly, smoothly. It was like being on ice. I picked up a remote, waited until the RV was oriented in the right direction, and then gave it a gentle squeeze. We were moving—at maybe ten miles an hour—south and west, toward the highway.

Off to my right, a helicopter approached. White letters on the side read "WSB." A traffic copter.

Chapter 18
HOME OF THE BRAVES

The red light gave Jim Stevens a thirty-second warning. He leaned forward and spoke into the mic. "It's a beautiful evening for a ball game here in Hotlanta as Nuenez prepares to throw out the first pitch."

Stevens paused for a moment, watching the pitcher rub his hand on his leg.

"Nuenez had a bit of a rough outing the last time he faced this Phillies lineup, so he's hoping to earn some redemption tonight. And now he takes the mound. The wind... the stretch... swung on! Fly ball. Perez goes deep in center. This will be an easy out. And... Oh! He drops it! Smith rounds first... what is Perez doing? The ball's just sitting there! Smith is on his way to third! Heyward and Schaefer are on their way to get the ball. This might be—"

And then he saw it.

"Holy *bleep*! What is *that?*"

A bus was rotating slowly in the air, just above the stadium lights. A camper? There was a man on top, scrambling around, with no visible safety wires.

"Wow! Ladies and gentlemen, this is... this is... well, it's a pretty amazing stunt. A spectacular optical illusion! It really looks as if there's a bus—you heard that right, a *bus*—just floating above the stadium. I can see some helicopters in the sky, but none of them seem to be positioned right for cables to suspend that thing."

There was a brief silence as Stevens just looked on in awe.

"Man! This really is an amazing stunt. These people are going to be in deep, deep trouble, but they're also gonna be rock stars. I'm telling you, this is absolutely, absolutely amazing. It'll be all over the news. I have no idea how they're doing this. It's just unbelievable. This is—wait a sec—hang on—now it looks like they're unfurling some kind of banner. Yep, a banner."

Stevens squinted his eyes. "Folks, it's a web address. And trust me, every single person in this entire stadium is pulling this up on their phones right now. The address is…"

www.DIYgravity.com

+++

Psst! Hey you. Yes, you... *the reader!* Dale's website is real. Hint, hint.

+++

ABOUT THE AUTHOR

I was born at Emory University Hospital and spent most of my life in Atlanta. Eventually I met and married the most beautiful kindergarten teacher in the whole world. Today we live in Florida with three wild little dudes, ages four, six, and eight. Our home is littered with toys and always very noisy.

You can contact me here:
mittywalters1@gmail.com

For a current list of my work, check here:
Mitty-Walters.com/more-by-mitty

Other ways to connect with me here:
Facebook: facebook.com/mitty.walters1
Website/Blog: Mitty-Walters.com
Twitter: twitter.com/MittyWalterz

***

If you enjoyed this book, would you please go back to where you got it and share your experience with others by leaving a review? Leaving a review is super easy and will only take a moment!

***

Made in the USA
Las Vegas, NV
17 June 2023

73568495R00115